STICKS & STONES

Abby Cooper

SQUARE FISH
FARRAR STRAUS GIROUX
NEW YORK

Readers: sticks and stones may break your bones, but words don't have to hurt. This is for you.

An imprint of Macmillan Publishing Group, LLC
175 Fifth Avenue
New York, NY 10010
mackids.com

Printed in the United States of America by LSC Communications, Harrisonburg, Virginia.

Library of Congress Cataloging-in-Publication Data
Names: Cooper, Abby.
Title: Sticks & stones / Abby Cooper.
Other titles: Sticks and stones
Description: New York : Farrar Straus Giroux, 2016. | Summary: Twelve-year-old Elyse has a rare genetic disorder that makes the words other people say about her appear on her body.
Identifiers: LCCN 2015039454 | ISBN 978-1-250-11526-3 (paperback) ISBN 978-0-374-30289-4 (ebook)
Subjects: | CYAC: Self-acceptance—Fiction. | Friendship—Fiction. | Diseases—Fiction. | Middle schools—Fiction. | Schools—Fiction. | BISAC: JUVENILE FICTION / Fantasy & Magic. | JUVENILE FICTION / Social Issues / Friendship.
Classification: LCC PZ7.1.C6477 St 2016 | DDC [Fic]—dc23
LC record available at http://lccn.loc.gov/2015039454

Originally published in the United States by Farrar Straus Giroux
First Square Fish edition: 2017
Square Fish logo designed by Filomena Tuosto

7 9 10 8 6

AR: 4.8 / LEXILE: 750L

TABLE OF CONTENTS

• • • • •

STICKS & STONES

1
WORDS

SOME PEOPLE DON'T THINK THAT ONE WORD CAN MAKE A difference.

They're wrong.

Sure, some words need to be around other words to make sense. They need to hang out together in a book or a song or a text message, or else you're stuck wrinkling your nose like *HUH? That doesn't make any sense.*

But some words don't need others. They have big-time serious meaning all by themselves.

I knew that better than anyone.

Like when it came to talking about me going to middle school this year. Mom said it would be *different*. Dr. Patel said it would be *challenging*. Dad said it would be *fine*.

They just needed one word each to sum up what they

thought a whole year would be like . . . and, so far, they were right.

One word nobody used, though? *Mysterious.*

And right now, that was the most important word of all.

I reached into my pocket and dug around until I found the folded blue paper again. Maybe it was a letter from a secret admirer or a gift certificate to Soup Palace, otherwise known as the Best Place on Earth.

Maybe it was nothing at all.

But it had to be *something*. It had my name on the front, after all, and was taped to my locker. I was dying to open it, but even if I found a way to read it sneakily, Ms. Sigafiss would probably see me and read it to everyone or rip it up or something. And that was if she was in a *good* mood.

I looked around the room, thinking about words.

Different.

Challenging.

Fine.

Mysterious.

They were just words, but they could change my whole life.

In fact, they already had.

2

LURCHES AND LETTERS

IF THERE WAS ONE PERSON WHO COULD MAKE ME FORGET about words and mysterious notes for a second, it was Liam. Dumb, beautiful, horrible, amazing Liam. I may have been a little confused about how I felt, but the one thing I knew for sure was that one quick look into his greenish-brownish eyeballs as he entered the classroom made me completely forget everything. It also made my heart get all lurchy and poundy, which I seriously did not appreciate. Was this feeling really necessary *every single time* I saw him? I pulled my pink polka-dot scarf up over my face before anyone could see the major redness that usually followed lurchy heart. *Not* a good look for school.

Like I had done the past few days, I tried my very hardest to think about something un-lurchworthy.

Sitting in Chicago traffic when we go to Dr. Patel's. Actually being at Dr. Patel's. This class. Boring, boring, boring. Perfect.

But then Jeg shot me a sideways glance from the seat next to me and Liam started chatting with Snotty Ami and my heart lurched all over again, big-time, and not in the overly excited kind of way. More like in the I-really-don't-like-this-one-bit kind of way.

I returned Jeg's look. "This stinks," I whispered.

"Totally," she said.

"Quiet!" Ms. Sigafiss rapped on her desk with a ruler.

She usually scared the bejeebers out of me, but at this moment she was my hero. *Anyone* who could make Liam and Snotty Ami stop talking to each other was automatically an awesome person, even if that person always wore frilly clothes and was permanently cranky.

"For the last ten minutes of class, please take out the assignment you began yesterday and continue working," she said.

I picked up my pencil and tried my hardest to concentrate on the paper in front of me, but it was way less blue and mysterious than the paper I really wanted to look at. And it was *much* less greenish-brownish than those awesome/evil eyeballs of Liam's that I wanted to look at but probably shouldn't look at.

Just write, I told myself. *You have to. Just do it already.*

So, finally, I did.

Hey, Future Self:

It's currently the first Thursday of sixth grade, and I'm sitting here in English class trying to write this, but I can't stop thinking about that folded paper. I wish I had noticed it sooner and had time to open it before class started because now there's nothing I can do and I might explode if I don't find out what it says soon. But no, I have to be patient and wait. And I will. (I'll definitely try my best to wait, at least. I think that should totally count for something.)

I'm supposed to write my goals for the year in this letter, and I think Ms. Sigafiss probably means English class goals, like read five thousand books and be a good listener and put all my commas in the right places, school stuff like that.

I definitely care about that stuff—reading and listening and commas—but it's not everything. So here are my actual goals:

1. *Stop thinking about the folded paper until I can finally open it after class.*

2. Stop obsessing over Liam, because he is done liking me.
3. Instead, obsess over boys like Nice Andy who **do** seem to like me.
4. Stop thinking about the folded blue paper until it's time to open it. (But for real this time, because I totally didn't stop the first time I told myself to stop. Have you stopped by now?)

Also, Future Me, I'm dying to know—is Jeg still your best friend? Has Dad spoken to you recently about anything that actually matters? Did Dr. Patel ever find a cure? Did you pass sixth grade? You better have. We are not going to be here two years in a row. We're just not. No pressure.

From,
September Self

P.S.: Sooo, what was that little blue paper all about??

The bell rang right as I finished my letter. Without wasting a second, I stuck my notebook in my purse, jumped out of my seat, scurried past Liam and his awesome/evil eyeballs, and sped right out into the hall.

Finally. I'd made it through class, and now it was finally, *finally* time. It felt like I had been waiting my whole twelve years of life for this, not just the past forty-five minutes, which was how long it had actually been since I'd first yanked the paper off my locker right as the you're-totally-going-to-be-late bell rang.

I took a ginormous deep breath, reached into my pocket, pulled out the blue paper, and opened it up.

Holy. High. Heels.

3
EXPLORER LEADER

BEFORE I COULD READ A WORD, SOMEONE CAME UP BEHIND me and snatched the paper right out of my hands.

"Excuse you," Jeg said with a smile. "What happened to reading that with your BFF?"

Busted.

"I was waiting for you! I was just opening it so it would be ready by the time you finished talking to everybody and got out here." Jeg was friends with everyone, but she was *best* friends with me. We had the necklaces to prove it and everything.

"Let's open it in the bathroom," she said. "You never know who could be watching and listening out here. It could be dangerous."

I rolled my eyes at her. "You're killing me," I said. Actually, the hallway was killing me. It was jam-packed and everyone walked like they were *trying* to take forever. We'd never make it to the bathroom at this rate.

"Why is everyone walking so slowly?" I asked.

"Um, hello . . ." Jeg gestured toward the walls.

Oh.

OH.

The hallway walls, normally very plain and white and boring, had been covered from floor to ceiling with all kinds of banners and posters advertising the sixth-grade trip we'd take later in the year. It wasn't till February, but everybody knew that it was a *huge* deal. After lots of competitions, one Explorer Leader would be chosen out of everybody in the grade. That person would be the boss of the trip and basically be famous for the rest of forever.

Jeg and I kept walking. We passed posters with photos of past Explorer Leaders, and everyone was stopping to take a look. Last year was Cody, who was grinning widely, clutching his official Explorer Leader certificate. The year before was Jordan, wearing a crown made out of leaves and beaming like she was Miss America. People had written messages on the posters around their faces. There were tons and tons of them. Even if I had the whole day to stand around and read, I would never have time to finish.

Cody = best E.L. EVER!!!

Jord, you did amazing. ♡

Best trip ever! Thanks Gabriela, you rule ü

On and on it went until we came to the poster for our class.

Except for an outline of a head and neck with a big question mark in the middle, the poster was totally blank. People were talking in loud, excited voices and straining their necks to have the best view of the empty sign.

"This is all yours, girl!" Lindsey said to Snotty Ami.

"I wonder who it will be," a guy I didn't know said to a girl I didn't know.

Everywhere I turned, people were buzzing about the posters, the trip, and how awesome and important the Explorer Leader was. The whole thing made me weirdly nervous. Maybe it was just because of all the people in the hall. The hallways in elementary school were never this crowded. There was always plenty of room to walk around and, you know, breathe. Here, there were like triple the people. Sometimes it was exciting, but most of the time I just felt squished.

"C'mon," Jeg said, pulling me by the arm. "Nobody

will be in the bathroom right now. We can come back and look more later."

I happily let myself be dragged away. Jeg always knew what I wanted without me having to tell her.

But only a minute later, just as I was *finally* about to read the paper, Snotty Ami pranced into the bathroom like she owned the place. Her hair—long, wavy, and the perfect shade of Little Mermaid red—lay flat against the little bumps poking out of her chest.

"Jeggie!" she said. "I thought I saw you come in here." Then she said, "Oh, hey, Elyse," in a *much* less excited voice.

"Hi, Ami." I tried not to notice how Jeg had turned her attention to the mirror. Out of the corner of my eye, I watched her grab a few things from her purse—*makeup* things. I had never seen her carry makeup things around before, and especially not use them. Before my brain could fully understand what was happening, she had smeared on a thick layer of red lipstick (since when did Jeg like lipstick?) and was starting to douse her face in shimmery gold glitter.

"Jeggie, you look fab," Snotty Ami said. "But your hair would be way cuter without those nasty pink streaks. It's such a pretty black and we can hardly even see it. We should totes go to the salon together sometime and take care of it."

"Totes," Jeg said.

I gave her a look, but she was staring at her strappy sandals like they were more interesting than my mysterious paper. Did she think I'd be mad to hear her talking like Snotty Ami? I wasn't, really. I just had a stomach that suddenly felt a little twisty.

Snotty Ami smiled snottily. "I'm gonna go look at Explorer Leader stuff. Wanna come, Jeggie?"

"I, um . . ." Jeg looked from me to Snotty Ami and back again. "I mean, would you mind, Elyse? Or you could come with us."

"But what about . . ." I paused as Snotty Ami leaned in. I swear, she and her posse (Jeg and I call them the Loud Crowd) have some kind of radar when you're about to tell a secret. Well, she wasn't going to know about this. "That thing?" I whispered. "That we were going to discuss? Here? Now?"

"Yeah, but I'll hurry, I promise. I'll just go peek at the stuff in the hall with Ami and then come right back, okay?"

"Um, okay, I guess."

Snotty Ami linked her arm through Jeg's.

"Seriously, I'll be right back," Jeg said to me. Then she winked, like she knew we still had a very important secret. Like she hadn't forgotten. Like everything was going to be okay and this was just temporary makeup-induced weirdness. Like her makeup, this would wear off by the end of the day.

"Later, dork!" Snotty Ami laughed, and practically pushed Jeg out the door.

I scratched my arm through my sleeve. It itched something major. And made me feel majorly pathetic, too. Maybe I *was* a little pathetic.

Jeg was the one who was supposed to protect me from words like *dork*, to stop the itching before it happened. But she said she'd come back, so she'd come back, and she'd help make it better.

My knees didn't seem to believe that, though. They felt wobbly, like they couldn't hold my legs up anymore, so I plopped down on a corner of the bathroom bench and scrunched myself up into a little ball. I leaned my head back against the cold tile and let out a long breath. Maybe Jeg couldn't help being weird. If Snotty Ami decided I was cool all of a sudden, I bet I would start acting weird, too.

I realized I was still clutching the paper, so I gently opened my fist and unfolded it. Sorry, Jeg. I'd tell her what it said when we chatted online after school.

Hi Elyse,

the inside said in teeny tiny typed letters.

Hello, paper.

I know who you are, and I know what you're dealing with. I want to help.

I blinked once. Twice. Then three times. Then a thousand times.

If you're ready for a change, show me by attending the meeting for Explorer Leader hopefuls tomorrow night. You'd make a great leader, you know . . . and giving it a shot would be good for you, too.

That was how it ended. No signature, no contact info, no nothing. I blinked about a zillion more times, and when I finally opened my eyes for real, the paper was still there.

Well, then. So much for a secret admirer or a gift certificate to the Best Place on Earth. (A coupon would have also been nice.)

And yet, interesting.

I stuffed the note back in my pocket, a gazillion thoughts flying through my brain. Who wrote this? And when? And why?

When I'd first heard about Explorer Leader, my brain

had said a big *No way.* It said, *Stay under the radar, Elyse. You don't need all hundred and fifty sixth graders knowing who you are.* But did this mysterious note have a point? It seemed like people usually loved the Explorer Leader and gave that person tons and tons of compliments. If I was the Explorer Leader, they'd probably write lots of good words on that blank poster, and I could read them again and again for the rest of forever. I could get a copy and hang it in my room. Take it on trips. Take it to college. Take it *everywhere.* Forever.

I sighed, still kinda bummed that Jeg had missed this. She probably just couldn't get out of Snotty Ami's snotty grasp in time. Plus, Jeg was always running late. Just last week, her cousins were in town from China and she was late meeting them for dinner. They had come from *another country.* And she had come from the mall.

So. Timeliness was not her specialty. They forgave her. I would, too. I always did.

But there was someone else out there who really cared about me. And *knew* about me. And didn't want me to feel like a dork ever again.

And that person was someone I wanted to know.

4

BEAUTIFUL

THERE WAS ONE MORE THING I HAD TO DO BEFORE I LEFT the bathroom.

No, not *that*. Nobody actually uses the bathroom in middle school.

Instead, I rolled my sleeve up to my elbow, and there it was, as expected: **D-O-R-K**. The bold, black word itched more than a thousand mosquito bites. I gave it a long scratch. *Ahhh*. Scratching felt good, but not good enough. Never good enough.

I took a big deep breath, trying to remember the good old days when getting itchy wasn't a problem. Maybe those days had never even existed for me. According to Mom and Dad, we first saw Dr. Patel when I was barely a week old. My regular doctor told them to make the drive from Indiana to Chicago to see him because he was a specialist, and even though I was just a baby who only knew how to poop and spit and burp and sleep, I was already a person who needed a special doctor.

The problem was that I was a beautiful baby, at least according to the doctor who helped Mom give birth to me. Normally that wouldn't be a bad thing, but when they saw **BEAUTIFUL** appear on my little baby arm moments after he said it in the delivery room, everybody was pretty freaked out. After all, babies are just supposed to *be* beautiful, not have the word plastered on their arms like a weird baby tattoo.

Then came the tests. Lots of tests. On me. On Mom. On the word. And then Dr. Patel said the three letters that would change my life forever: C-A-V. CAV. Short for *cognadjivisibilitis*. Short for *freakiest freaky disorder ever.*

Then he said, *Hey, you guys should move to Chicago so I can be your doctor forever and ever and ever. Because you're going to need me forever. Because you're going to have CAV forever. Stinks to be you!*

He may not have really said that. I don't remember.

It would have been cool if I could've just stayed beautiful forever. But no—kids had other plans for me, and none of them were good.

Now my thoughts and eyes shifted back to the massive **DORK** on my arm. I let out a quiet whimper, knowing I'd be stuck with this itchy thing for the next two to four weeks before it faded. Longer, if someone said it again. And with Snotty Ami butting in on my Jeg time—and never missing a chance to be her snotty self—it was totally possible that she would be the one to repeat it.

I rolled my sleeve back down quickly so that no one would come in and see my arm. As the fabric reached my fingers, I realized that my other arm was kinda itchy, too. *Huh?*

I bit my lip. It didn't make any sense for my other arm to be itchy. Snotty Ami had only called me **DORK**, and no one had called me anything else too bad lately. I knew it had to be a bad word because only the bad ones itched. Plus, the letters usually formed one by one like someone was writing them on my skin with a sharp fingernail. But that hadn't happened. Or maybe it did, but I was too busy wondering about the note to notice. I guess that was possible.

I rocked back and forth and rubbed my sweaty hands on my pants. *Just look,* I told myself. *How bad can it be?* Also, *When did my hands get so sweaty?*

I rolled up the sleeve, my heart racing. The word was horizontal, so I saw it all at once: **PATHETIC**.

Pathetic?

I tilted my head to the side and thought back to

earlier in the day. No, Snotty Ami hadn't called me pathetic. Nor had Jeg or Liam or Ms. Sigafiss or anybody else.

But then I sat up very straight and pressed my palms to my cheeks as I remembered something important. There *was* one person who'd called me pathetic: *me*.

For a second it felt like I was glued to the bench. I couldn't move a muscle or think or talk or even breathe. The world stood completely still. This was *not* one of Freaky Thing's symptoms. I *knew* it wasn't. CAV meant itchy bad words and soothing good words. It meant being careful about who I hung out with so that I heard more good than bad. It meant always watching out for what other people called me.

It had never before meant watching out for what I called myself.

Holy. High. Heels.

Dr. Patel was going to love this one. I could already see the headline: "New Symptom of CAV Discovered! Still No Cure in Sight. Elyse Doomed Forever."

I stared out into space as I pushed my sleeve back down. The bathroom looked exactly like it had a few minutes ago, but everything was different. I had a note and a new secret, and I had them both before second period.

It was going to be a long day.

5

POOPYHEAD

I COULDN'T TELL MOM OR DAD ABOUT THE NEW SYMPTOM, even though keeping it to myself was driving me crazy. But being driven a little crazy was way better than being driven to Dr. Patel's at a gazillion miles per hour, which was exactly what my parents would do if they knew. This would totally freak them out, and one freaked-out person in the family was more than enough. I could probably handle it myself anyway. At least, I hoped I could.

After dinner the next night, Mom and I went to my room so she could help make my hair cute for the meeting. With each brush stroke, I almost blurted out, *Guess what? Now the names I call myself show up on my arms and legs, too! Isn't that just delightful?* But luckily Mom started talking before I could get myself in more trouble.

"My friend Veronika's daughter was Explorer Leader,"

Mom said. "She had a great experience. No matter what happens, I'm proud of you for trying this, sweetie. Just remember, sticks and stones . . ."

She didn't have to finish the saying because I knew it backwards and forwards. She had told me every night before bed since I was little. *Sticks and stones may break my bones, but words will never hurt me.*

Words did hurt me, though. Well, itched me. Close enough.

I shuddered, thinking of the words bugging me now and all the ones that had bugged me before. Then I giggled to myself a tiny bit, remembering the first bad name I had ever been called. The one that changed everything.

It happened at preschool. Mom stayed with me the whole first day, holding my hand the entire time and only letting certain kids get near me. But the one time she left the room for a second, Max Iverson came up to me and called me the worst name you could possibly be called in preschool: poopyhead. That's all it took.

When Mom came back, I was surrounded by kids and teachers and was screaming my brains out. **POOPYHEAD** took up a huge chunk of my forearm. And it itched. Bad. Bad bad bad bad bad. The only good thing was that Jeg was sitting right beside me, scratching it like it was a fun game, like it was totally normal to see a word on a person's body and even more normal to plop down next to that person and scratch it. Well, Mom plucked me up right out of the crowd, threw me over her shoulder, and whisked me off to the doctor before I could say goodbye to any of my new friends. (Or get revenge on that Max kid.)

I don't remember much about the appointment, but I remember Dr. Patel. After he examined me for what felt like hours, poking and prodding and grimacing and groaning, he said, "Don't worry, Elyse. It'll get easier with time."

But it didn't. It got harder. I thought he was full of baloney, and not the delicious kind you put in a sandwich.

At least when I went back to preschool the day after the Poopyhead Incident, the super-wise four-year-old Jeg decided that she would become my personal bodyguard to prevent any more icky comments. Mom has all these hilarious videos where you can see little Jeg—usually wearing a floppy hat, a poofy tutu, and a pair of silky princess pajama pants all at the same time—standing right in front of me with her little hands on her hips, a fierce expression in her eyes. When kids wanted to play with me, she'd ask, "Do you promise to say only nice things?" and the kids had to swear on their stuffed animals that they would.

After the Poopyhead Incident, Mom would go to school with me every day and wait until Jeg got there. When Jeg took off her coat and went into bodyguard mode, Mom finally went home.

Jeg didn't ask people to swear on their stuffed animals once we started elementary school, but she still looked out for me.

Most of the time.

I pushed the memory aside as Mom looped a rubber band around the end of my French braid. She left me to get dressed for the meeting, and I thought about the blue note again. Whoever had written it had made a good point: being Explorer Leader—and getting those great words—would be awesome for me. The writer was wrong about one thing, though: it *could* hurt to try.

But I think I wanted to try anyway.

6

THE WEIRD KIND OF WEIRD

I TOOK MY TIME TO FINISH GETTING READY, WANTING TO make sure my outfit was as perfect as it could be. I pulled on my comfiest socks, the pink ones with the silver stars on them, and then tried on lots of different accessories before settling on a fun silver charm bracelet and my half of the Best Friends necklace Jeg gave me for my tenth birthday. It was part of her famous-fashion-designer parents' jewelry collection, and they were super-funky designers. They were so funky, in fact, that they had started calling their daughter Jeg, instead of her real name, Jenny, when jeggings first became a thing. She looked so awesome in their jegging line. The name couldn't have suited her any better, and it's stuck ever since.

I fastened the necklace around my neck and rubbed

the charm between my fingers. Instead of just saying *Best* or *Friends* like every other friendship necklace in the world, it was this artsy peace-sign shape that looked really cool whether it was attached to the other person's necklace or not. It was one of my most prized possessions.

I grabbed my favorite fruity perfume from my dresser and gave myself a little spritz. As I set it back down, something else caught my eye—a single piece of gum. A gift from Liam. Ugh. I should have gotten rid of that thing months ago, or at least chewed it while it was still chewable. Now it was probably a gross, moldy mess, just like my heart.

When Liam and I first started going out at the end of fifth grade, he told me all these weird secrets about himself, like how he still slept with a stuffed animal (Mr. Koala Snuggles) and once kept a piece of gum in a jar as a pet named Chewy. (That's why he gave me gum: not in case I wanted minty-fresh breath, but in case I wanted a pet.) And, in his spare time, he liked to bake pies out of cheese puffs, cereal, and French fries, just to see what would happen when he put them in the oven. So weird. So awesome. So awesomely weird.

And then I showed him my words. Like everyone else at our elementary school, he knew about them, but he was one of the few people who really liked seeing them up close and wanted to know more about them. He'd ask me questions all the time.

"How'd you get it?"

"Nobody knows, Liam. Something about a bad gene my mom passed on."

"How many people have it?"

"Beats me. I don't know of anyone else. Dr. Patel says it's one of the rarest disorders in the world."

"Why are they only on your arms and legs? Why are some big and some small?"

"Because that's where they show up. And that's just how they form. I never know where one will pop up or what size it'll be."

I never had real answers to his questions, since there was a lot Dr. Patel was still researching. Dr. Patel spent lots of time researching, but the truth was that he couldn't really do much to make me better or change anything. Mainly we just talked and he made me feel less like a weirdo. I told Liam this, but he kept asking things anyway. He thought it was interesting.

Like me, he wasn't totally normal.

It was fantastic.

On our sixth and last day of going out, my heart pounded extra hard when I saw him and I didn't know why. It was more than my regular OMG-he's-so-cute-and-weird-in-a-good-way-and-I-can't-handle-it lurchy heart. It was the kind where I thought my heart was going to jump out of my body, run down the street, and never come back.

"This is going to be the last time we hang out," Liam said. He crossed his arms and I felt like someone had kicked me so hard that all my insides fell out. Like I had nothing inside of me. Like I was a big blob of empty nothingness.

"Middle school starts this fall," he said, like I didn't know, but I actually knew very well. In fact, I had day-dreams about us walking down the hallway hand in hand all romantically like people in middle school probably did. Liam would lead the way, showing people my words and looking out for me like Jeg always did. With two awesome bodyguards by my side, the words would definitely be all amazing, all the time.

"Yeah . . . middle school. So?" My voice was shaky.

"So . . ." He squirmed. "I can't really be associated with . . ." He gestured to me. "All your weird stuff. It's too weird. You were really interesting to hang out with, though."

WEIRD popped up and itched like I knew it would, but when **INTERESTING** formed, it didn't feel like much. Maybe my CAV wasn't sure, like I wasn't, whether that word was a compliment or a diss. Usually words like that didn't feel like much at all.

"It's just, in middle school, the CAV stuff, it's not . . . I can't. My brother told me it's gonna be different. And I want to have more time this summer for soccer and Kevin and the guys, anyway. We can still be friends, though. I'll text you. Trust me, you don't really wanna be with me."

I was pretty sure I did, actually.

That's all he said before he walked away and left me by myself, scratching **WEIRD** and wondering what I did wrong.

Jeg, busy that day with another friend, wasn't there to help me scratch the word or to stop it from happening in the first place.

And Liam, the one who used to think weird was cool, had caused it.

I tried to get home right away, since I was technically supposed to be walking home with Liam and not by myself, but when I passed the Oak Park Public Library, I had to take a break to sit on a bench and scratch. When I looked up, I saw a whole bunch of kids I didn't recognize. They looked like they were about my age, but they must have been from a different elementary school.

And after all the commotion of Liam leaving and me crying and itching and freaking out, they were staring at me like I was nuts.

I gulped and wrapped myself in a hug, like I was a

little animal trying to protect myself from predators. Kids from my school knew they weren't allowed to call me bad names, but kids from other schools didn't know me and didn't know the rules. Whenever I'd see people I didn't know out at the mall, the library, the pool, wherever, I'd have someone with me. A friend. Mom. Dad. *Someone.* And they'd give the strangers scary looks, and they'd cover my ears if it looked like someone was going to say something bad.

But this time I was alone.

"What's wrong with your arms and legs?" some kid with spiky hair and glasses asked. I was already crying a little bit, but that was enough to push me over the edge. My arms flailed away from my body as I cried and cried and cried.

"What'd you do to that freak, Felix?" A girl came up to the boy.

FREAK formed on my kneecap right before their eyes.

"Holy meatballs!" yelled Felix. "What are you, some kind of a witch?"

"Witch!" the girl repeated, laughing.

WITCH was itchy. So, so itchy. I was an itchy, itchy witchy.

The rest of their friends approached. Before they could say anything, I scrambled away as quickly as I could.

As I ran home that day, tears streaming down my

cheeks and words itching the bejeebers out of my body, I realized: maybe Mom, Dad, Jeg, and Liam were the only people who thought CAV was cool. And now Liam *didn't* think it was cool, and Jeg wasn't around as much, so maybe she didn't, and Mom and Dad . . . Well, parents *had* to tell you that you were cool, even if you weren't. Everybody knew that.

If this was a sign of what people really thought when they weren't being threatened by my parents or friends or teachers, then, well, maybe CAV wasn't the cool kind of weird after all. Maybe it was the weird kind of weird, plain and simple.

So I decided, right then and there on that sticky almost-summer day, that I could never wear shorts or T-shirts ever again. And, throughout the summer, I had stuck to my promise. Even if I was hot all the time.

Hot was better than itchy.

7

IT'S ON

"ELYSE, WE GOTTA GO!"

I took one last look at the gum and decided I'd throw it out later. Then I hurried downstairs and joined Mom and Dad in the car.

"This class trip is going to be so great for you, sweetie," Mom said as she put on her seat belt. "I know it's months away, but I made some lists. Things you have, things you need, things you don't have that you might need, types of anti-itch cream that are best for cold weather . . ."

I groaned. Prescription anti-itch cream was the only thing that made my bad CAV words feel better, but the stuff was seriously nasty. Not only was it thick and gooey, but it also smelled like milk somebody should've thrown away weeks ago.

Mom passed a notebook back to me, and I held it up

in front of the window and pretended to read her lists. Really, though, I just wanted to look out the window.

"Don't worry about all this stuff, Elyse," Dad said. "You'll be fine. It'll be good. Everything's good."

Mom rubbed his shoulder for a second, and then turned back to look at me. "Of course everything is good. Well, that's what we're aiming for. But we have to be prepared. Sometimes things don't go how we want them to. I have lotion for tonight in my purse, just in case things get itchy in there. Okay?"

I stared back out the window, pretending I hadn't heard her. Maybe if I didn't think about the possibility of things going wrong, they wouldn't.

Dad changed the subject. "So, anything interesting happen in school lately?"

"Not really." I considered it. *Not really* was usually not good enough of an answer for my parents, especially when it came to school stuff. "Well, Ms. Sigafiss had us write letters to ourselves. We have to do it in a notebook every month, and then we get to read them someday in the future. And she doesn't even read them! She just kind of flips through every now and then to see that we did it."

"That *is* cool!" Mom's voice got all high and excited. "What did you write?"

"Um . . . it's private."

If Mom knew that I had gotten a mysterious blue

note—and that most of my letter to myself was me wondering what it said—she'd totally freak out.

"Oh, okay," she said. She sounded a little disappointed, but then she perked up again. "Still. Really cool project, sweetie."

We parked and walked into the school auditorium from the big lot. Our principal, Mr. Todd, stood at a small podium on the stage, and almost everyone I knew—plus a bunch of people I didn't know—sat in the audience. This many people wanted to be Explorer Leader? My heart sank all the way to the ground. Lower, if possible. There was no way I'd get picked when there was this much competition.

Besides all the people in my grade, there were parents, brothers, sisters, teachers, everybody. Even Ms. Sigafiss was there, sitting in the back row with all our other teachers, the typical I-hate-everything frown plastered across her face. It looked like most people were sitting with their families, so Mom, Dad, and I grabbed a few seats together toward the back. I looked around for Jeg and her parents. They were up near the very front, right next to—was that Snotty Ami? It was, and she was all by herself. No parents or anything. Well, that was totally unfair. I was about to ask Mom if it would be okay if I moved to sit by them when Mr. Todd started talking.

"Welcome, students, parents, teachers, and friends!" His voice boomed out across the room. "I want to thank you all for taking a short time out of your Friday evening for this important meeting. Parents, you're here because your child is interested in being the Explorer Leader of the annual sixth-grade trip to Minnesota this February. Though there will be only one leader, I like to think of that person as a representative of our whole community of sixth graders and their families. We're all a team, which is why we learn together, grow together, and support each other at events like tonight's meeting."

The room buzzed with energy, excitement, and nerves (if you were me). What was I doing here? I didn't belong here. I belonged at home, where it was safe.

Mr. Todd continued, "The Explorer Leader will have enormous responsibility in the planning and implementing of activities on the trip. This person will be organized, creative, and able to take charge. This person will also be well versed in the arts of physical and mental endurance. As you can tell from the overwhelming attendance at this meeting, dozens of students feel they have these very qualities. I will select a small committee of students to serve as Explorer Helpers, but only one will be chosen as the leader."

I leaned back in my seat and watched Mr. Todd while he kept talking for what felt like years. His longish hair flopped around when he moved, which was a lot. Mr. Todd was almost as excited about this as we were.

I started paying attention again right as he said, "I'll be conducting interviews in early October with the students who have the best attendance and grades between now and then, and the selection process will continue from there. One lucky student will be guaranteed a free pass into this interview round . . ." He paused and smiled like he had a secret. "And that's the student who wins the brief competition we're going to have right now. Students, please make your way to the stage."

What? My whole body felt tingly as the room began to buzz again. This was supposed to be a meeting, not a contest. I knew there would be contests, of course—everyone knew there would be contests. But no one had said they were going to start tonight.

I caught Jeg's eye as I stumbled my way up to the stage. She didn't want to be Explorer Leader, but she had come to the meeting anyway to hang out with me—or maybe to hang out with Snotty Ami. It was a little hard to tell, if I was being honest. But the place *was* packed—maybe they didn't sit together on purpose. Maybe Snotty Ami had to grab any old seat she could get, and it happened to be that one.

Once we were all assembled on the stage, Mr. Todd turned back to the audience. "Being the Explorer Leader can be challenging at times. The student will get tired, frustrated, and downright crabby. But he or she must remember that this is a job worth having and fighting for. Tonight, we'll see who wants it the most. Students, upon my go, you will lift one foot in the air and hold the position as long as you can. The winner of this competition will be guaranteed a spot in the next round of the process that will lead to the selection of this year's Explorer Leader."

"Go, Elyse! You can do it!" shouted a way-too-familiar voice from the audience.

I refused to make eye contact with Mom and hoped with all my heart that everyone would think there was just some random lady in the audience cheering for me, a lady I didn't know at all who didn't have, like, twenty-eight thousand varieties of gross prescription anti-itch cream stashed in her purse in case of an emergency.

"Students ready?" Mr. Todd asked. "Oh, and, folks, please note that flash photography *is* permitted in our theater!" He grinned. Yes, this was hilarious. Let's totally embarrass kids and then invite people to record it. "Get set . . . go!"

And with that, we were off. I lifted my right foot slightly up off the stage floor. Okay, this wasn't so bad. I could do this. It was just standing. I did that all the time.

"Just so you know, I take dance and gymnastics," Snotty Ami hissed in my ear. "I could do this all night."

I ignored her and turned my body to the side. *Concentrate.* The seconds went by, and legs began to drop one by one. Kevin wobbled around for a minute before falling, and then a few other people lost their balance, too. My leg had grown a little heavy, but not heavy enough that I'd let it fall. Not heavy enough to give up this chance for nonstop compliments. I'd made it this long; I'd keep going.

Nice Andy flashed me a humongous grin, the kind where you could see all his teeth, even the big ones way back in his mouth. He looked like a statue, totally frozen in place.

A few more legs fell. *Don't get excited. Stay calm. Focus.*

My eyes wandered out to the crowd. Mom had her phone out and was probably taking a video of me to put online. So embarrassing. Liam sat a few rows behind my parents with some soccer-team guys and their families, and I could've been imagining it, but it definitely looked like he was smiling at me. Maybe he was thinking about how he had made a mistake, how he still thought my words were the cool kind of weird, and how we could totally go out again and hold hands in the hallway and do all those other romantic things people do when they're going out.

I forced myself to look away, though it sure wasn't easy. *No distractions. And absolutely no lurchy heart.* Not right now.

The time crawled on and on until I was convinced it was midnight.

"Ah!" Francheska fell to the side. She grabbed on to JaShawn, who grabbed on to Layla, who grabbed on to Elijah, who made them all fall down like a stack of dominoes.

Now it was down to Snotty Ami, Nice Andy, and, somehow, me. The crowd roared like we were in an epic battle for an Olympic gold medal.

"Wow!" Nice Andy whispered in his usual overly happy voice. "You're really good at this! Too bad I'm going to win!" He jumped up and down a few times as if to prove how talented he was at standing on one foot. But then, in only a split second, Nice Andy tripped over his own shoelace and landed in a heap on the floor. Everyone clapped politely.

"Whoops!" he said, laughing as he got up.

"And then there were two!" hollered Mr. Todd.

The Loud Crowd practically flew up to the stage.

"You got this, Ami!" Paige squealed.

"C'mon, girl!" Lindsey shrieked. She leaned in close. "You can't get beaten by a loser."

I squeaked as **LOSER** sprang up on my knee through my leggings.

"Oh, oops," Lindsey said, as if she'd just remembered she wasn't supposed to say stuff like that. "I was just kidding. It was, like, a funny loser, not a real one. Sorry."

She didn't sound very sorry.

I shot Jeg a look at the same time and couldn't help but notice her plain black hair. Snotty Ami worked fast; the pink streaks were all gone. It was like they had never even existed.

I hopped up and down on one foot in a circle, hoping that the hopping motion would somehow make **LOSER** go away. When all my hobbling around didn't make it better, I tried to reach down and scratch my knee without falling over. I probably looked like I was trying—and failing—to do that sprinkler dance that my dad always did when I had friends over.

I didn't have friends over too much these days.

"Oh, you want a dance-off?" Snotty Ami said. Before I knew what was happening, she was jumping up, spinning in a circle, and landing perfectly on one foot. "It's on."

I pretended I hadn't noticed any of it and kept my gaze focused into the audience straight ahead.

"Hey, El." Jeg came closer to me. "You're doing great."

"Thanks," I whispered. Then she moved past me and scooted over to join the Loud Crowd's clump. *Huh?*

LOSER itched again, making me feel awful. And if that wasn't bad enough, **DORK** and **PATHETIC** prickled my skin, too, like they were feeling left out and wanted some attention. I closed my eyes and tried to focus on breathing and forgetting about the itchy words.

It didn't work.

At. All.

Why is it that when you try to forget something, you only end up thinking about it more?

I really was **PATHETIC**. It had to be true. Otherwise Snotty Ami would want to be my friend like she wanted to be Jeg's friend. Otherwise Jeg wouldn't have gone to stand by the cool people instead of by me.

My whole body itched, even though only a couple of words were ruining it for the rest of me. It stung. Everything stung.

But it didn't have to. If the blue-note writer was right, I could be a really good Explorer Leader, and being Explorer Leader could be really good for me. As an added bonus, it sounded like it would make me really busy. Too busy to think about Liam, Jeg, Snotty Ami, or myself. And if I couldn't think about myself, then I definitely couldn't think about how pathetic I was.

And that was exactly what I needed.

Snotty Ami nudged me with her elbow, reminding me that I was still on a stage in front of everyone, fighting for a shot at something that might really make the itches go away forever.

“Give up yet, nerd?” she whispered.

NERD pinched my skin. I swallowed hard and stumbled back a little. Between **NERD**, **DORK**, **LOSER**, and **PATHETIC** all trying to out-itch each other, I was getting a little wobbly. I rolled my foot in circles and then hobbled around the stage, but it was no use. I was a doomed Jenga tower, leaning sideways until I had toppled over all the way to the floor.

“And that’s a wrap!” Mr. Todd hollered like he was announcing the final score of the Super Bowl. “Congratulations, Ami, you’ve made it one step closer to being the Explorer Leader! You have a guaranteed pass into the next round. And great job to all participants! Have a wonderful night, folks, and drive safe.”

I didn’t get up. Everything itched too much for me to move a muscle.

From my spot on the floor, I felt Snotty Ami’s snotty footsteps snottily sauntering away. The Loud Crowd followed her, giggling at the top of their lungs like they had some super-hilarious inside joke that regular people would never understand. Jeg paused for a second, stopping to look back at me. And just as I thought she was about to come over and help me up, she turned the other way and left.

She waved first.

But still.

She left.

"You okay down there? You did a great job, sweetie. That was a tough competition." Of course, I couldn't just lie here by myself for a minute. Mom stood over me, her ginormous purse in one hand and a life-size bottle of lotion in the other.

"Grrmrmrrrugh," I said, which meant *Of course I'm not okay! Does it* look *like I'm okay?* But Mom took it to mean, *Please roll up my sleeves and slather me with the smelliest anti-itch cream* ever *and totally embarrass me in front of everyone who's still here.*

"It's okay, sweetie," she said. "Right?" She elbowed Dad in the stomach. "You can still get the job. And you should be really proud of yourself for how long you lasted up there. Second place is fantastic!"

"Right." Dad glanced up from his phone for about a millisecond. "You did . . . you were . . . Hey, just think about something else for now. The average person eats thirty-five thousand cookies in their lifetime. That's pretty interesting stuff, don't you think?"

I answered with an eye roll. Cookies are awesome. Talking about cookies right this second? Not so much.

"You did a great job, Elyse," said Nice Andy. He was the only person left on the stage who wasn't related to me.

Yeah, so great, I thought sarcastically. *That's why I look like a ghost right now because of all this cream.*

Nice Andy, Mom, and Dad all smiled these huge, wide smiles at me that kinda made me want to cry more. *A whole bunch of other people lost, too,* I wanted to remind them. Why couldn't they go smile at someone else?

I knew they were just trying to be nice. And I liked nice, usually. I *needed* nice.

Times like this—when I'm surrounded by smiles I don't deserve—always made me think about chocolate frosting, for some reason. I ate a whole container of it once. It was the most amazing thing, at first. But after a while, it just made my stomach hurt.

That's how it was with me. People were either too mean or too nice. The only *real* people, the people who always acted good and normal, were Jeg and Liam. And now Liam was gone and Jeg was— Well, I didn't know what she was, but she wasn't here.

But maybe if I got Explorer Leader, she and Liam would give me some good words.

Slowly, I let Nice Andy pull me up.

I'd lost, but it wasn't over.

8

NICE ANDY

NICE ANDY AND I HAD BECOME FRIENDS ON THE FIRST DAY of kindergarten, when Dr. Patel came to my class during show-and-tell and talked about CAV. After everything that had happened in preschool, Mom and Dad thought it would be a good idea for him to come talk to the kids in my class, and I totally agreed that it was the most awesome idea ever. A real live person for show-and-tell totally beat a stuffed animal or a light-up race car or any of the other stuff people brought in, no contest. He told the class how CAV made a person very special, but sometimes you had to be careful around special things.

"Can we see it happen?" Liam had asked.

Dr. Patel looked at me, and I nodded. The class was pretty new to show-and-tell, but everyone already knew that you couldn't bring something amazing and then refuse to show how it worked. "Elyse is awesome!" he said.

The letters popped up on my wrist one by one. **A-W-E-S-O-M-E.** The entire class oohed and aahed. Best. Show-and-tell. Ever.

And then everyone started talking at once, and soon I was completely covered. **AMAZING. COOL. PRETTY. SUPER-DUPER. FUN. GREAT.**

Words popped up all over my arms and legs, and since you never know where on my arm or leg one will appear, my body suddenly became like a scavenger hunt. Kids jumped out of their seats to run around me in circles and point at things.

"I found **FUN**!" someone hollered from behind me. The word was right below my knee.

"**COOL** is over here!" Someone grabbed my arm and held it up for everyone to see. I laughed along with the group. Kindergarten was the best.

"Calm down," our teacher said. "Remember, Elyse is not a toy!" And then she said, in a very scary voice, that anyone who chose to call me a bad name would face serious consequences.

"Like no stickers?" Nice Andy asked, horrified.

"Like no stickers. Among other things."

And then the party ended a little bit, because we had forgotten all about the whole bad-words aspect of my amazing show-and-tell, and everyone got kinda depressed over the thought of no stickers ever again. Our teacher had given us really amazing scratch-and-sniff ones that morning, so it wasn't really a risk anyone wanted to take.

We had the same little show-and-tell session each year of elementary school. To remind people, I guess. It got a lot more boring as I got older. Dr. Patel just babbled on and on about CAV, and whatever teacher I had made the same serious-consequences statement. Stickers didn't matter as much as we got older, but there was always something that did.

On the first day of middle school, Mr. Todd had called me into his office to ask if I'd like him to keep the show-and-tell tradition going. He had already been filled in about CAV from old teachers and Dr. Patel.

Obviously the answer to that was a big fat no-thank-you. CAV used to be cool, but now it was embarrassing. If I just wore my long sleeves and my long pants, maybe everyone would forget I had it. I'd be called names because of them forgetting, probably, but being itchy was better than being embarrassed.

Mom found out I said no, of course, and *begged* me—practically forced me—to change my mind. The only way I could calm her down was to agree to carry a travel-size lotion at all times and put Dr. Patel on speed dial on my cell phone.

The only thing I'd miss about the class talks was getting a picture from Nice Andy afterward. I still had some of them. Once, he gave me a giant piece of paper that said "U R SO NIS" above a picture of two stick people holding hands, surrounded by hearts. After another show-and-tell, the paper said, "CAV is ok and grate" next to a picture of me in a cape that said "Super CAV Girl." In another, the line of nice words turned into a paragraph, and Super CAV Girl got eyebrows, pierced ears, a magic wand, a crown, and her own unicorn.

I used to show the pictures to Jeg. "Cool," she'd say. Then she'd say something like, "Let's go read a book. You can do the characters' voices. You're great at voices!"

Even though Jeg protected me from mean kids and bad words, she wasn't nice to me *because* I had CAV. She was nice to me just because that's how she was. Nice Andy made me great pictures. Smiled at me. Gave me compliments. But sometimes I wondered if he really knew anything about me at all.

9

STRING CHEESE

Hey, Self—

I'm baaaack! Did you miss me?

You probably remember this, but in case you don't, there was another blue piece of paper stuck to my locker yesterday. It was folded about a zillion times so it fit perfectly in the palm of my hand. Like the first one, the message inside was typed.

This time, though, I didn't wait for Jeg to tell me when it was okay to open it. (Remember?)

In fact, I didn't tell her about it at all.

Instead, I ripped it open right then and there, and it's taped in here so I can keep it forever.

Hi Elyse,

Here's an idea for you: stop thinking so much and *do things.* This will make you feel much better about yourself, and could lead to you getting chosen as Explorer Leader, too. Even though you lost the foot-in-the-air competition, you still have a chance!

It was an awesome note to get. So now I just have to do things and this person will make sure I get Explorer Leader. No problem.

Well, hopefully no problem. The truth is that the idea of doing more stuff makes my insides a little squirmy.

Mom knows something is up, because she keeps putting her face **way** too close to my face and asking, "Are you okay?" in that hushed tone where she knows something is seriously wrong but doesn't want to come right out and ask me what it is. (I hope she has stopped doing that by the time you read this someday.) The fact of the matter is, I feel pretty darn alone. I would have figured that out even if **LONER FREAK** hadn't sprouted across my leg last week when I was in the shower.

I have to stop thinking. I have to focus on doing things that will get Mr. Todd's attention.

That will show him that I'm the best choice—the only choice—for Explorer Leader, and for that giant compliment-filled poster. And it'll show the note writer, too.

Oh, and, Self, you should probably know that you started going out with Nice Andy. I mean, you do know, obviously. But are you still going out? I'm so curious! You probably remember the whole romantic story, but in case you need a refresher, it all started with string cheese (as all good romantic stories should, I think).

"Do you like cheese?" he asked one day after an especially frustrating hour of math with Mrs. Catalano, and I nodded eagerly because, duh, cheese is awesome. "I stole the string cheese from my little brother's lunch box! Major score! Okay, I asked him for it! But still, he said okay and I got some and here it is!" He handed over a package.

Now, here's a guy who appreciates me, I thought. Yeah, he is a little too nice, but he gave me cheese. Liam never gave me cheese. And the rest is history.

There is a chance that I might still like Liam, just a teeny tiny, microscopic little bit. I wouldn't admit that to anyone else but you. He may have never given me cheese, but he did give me gum. Plus, he's the weirdest guy I know, and the best. Besides Nice Andy, I mean.

Anyway, I don't know when you'll read this, but I hope things will be better then.

Goals:

1. Find out who's writing those notes!
2. Be nicer to Nice Andy because he is a real live guy who likes me and gives me cheese.
3. Stop caring about everything Liam says and does and also his overall existence.
4. Stop missing Jeg. She hardly talks to me now. She's too busy with her new friends.
5. Get some friends. (No, awesome books and/or socks do not count.)
6. Stop thinking so much and just do things—especially things that will help me become Explorer Leader.

Also, today I bought a pink-lemonade-flavored Chapstick and it looks excellent on me even though technically it is clear. I just thought you should know.

From,
October Self

• • •

I sat back in my seat as the morning announcements began.

"Hey there, it's your princi-*pal,* coming to you live from the front office." I could practically hear Mr. Todd grinning through the intercom. "A special message for sixth graders today—I want to give you fair warning that I'm almost finished reviewing your attendance and grade reports for the first month of school, and the students who come out on top will be interviewed for Explorer Leader sometime in the next few weeks. Congratulations to Ami Kowalski, who is guaranteed an interview after her win at the first competition. There are still five more spots up for grabs. I also want to remind you about the fund-raising show. November is not as far away as it seems! We have only a few acts signed up so far and would really like to get some more."

The fund-raising show had been announced on the first day of school. We could do anything we wanted, as long as it was appropriate and not that horrible to sit through—and people would have to pay five dollars to see it. All the money would be put toward our Minnesota trip.

People were excited about the show, but everyone knew it was one of those things that was really made for cool people to feel cooler and weird people to feel weirder, like school dances. Sure, I'd been playing piano forever and had performed in about a zillion recitals, but that didn't mean I needed to do it in front of everybody at school. If I signed up, the whole order of the universe would be messed up, and a lot of people would be really confused. I didn't want to be responsible for that kind of social destruction, so that would not be happening. But an interview with Mr. Todd? That, I would love to do.

The room started getting noisy after Mr. Todd finished the rest of his announcements, but Ms. Sigafiss held up a hand.

"Moving on. We're going to do another introduction." Ms. Sigafiss had started this on the first day of school. She said it was good for kids in middle school to get to know people from different elementary schools. I thought it was a pretty cool thing to do. After all, there were thirty-ish people in our class, and I only knew around ten of them. Maybe there were some nice people in English with me and I didn't even know it. "Today we will listen to Olivia," she said without even bothering to see whose hands were actually raised.

"Um, okay!" Olivia said. She stood and rubbed her hands on her faded jeans. "So I'm Olivia, which you already know . . . I went to Hoover Elementary. My best friends are my five brothers and sisters. My favorite sport is soccer, and my favorite colors are hot pink and turquoise."

Wow. She was really cool. I'd love to be friends with her, but would she want to be friends with me? And would I even be able to get a chance to talk to her before the Loud Crowd sucked her in?

While I was thinking about it, Lindsey had already complimented Olivia's shiny black hair (she wore it in lots of little braids running down her back with purple beads at the bottom), and now they were chatting away like they'd been best friends for a thousand years.

"Thanks, Olivia," Ms. Sigafiss said. "We'll do another one tomorrow."

"Can I go tomorrow?" Lindsey's hand shot up.

Ms. Sigafiss glared at her. "Maybe," she said.

Lindsey put her hand down and whispered something to Snotty Ami.

"Quiet!" Ms. Sigafiss grumbled. "No speaking unless you're spoken to." She grabbed a red dry-erase marker and started writing something on the whiteboard. "Get your response journals," she said without taking her eyes off the board. "We will be working on these questions silently for the next fifteen minutes."

We all made a beeline to the basket of journals in the corner of the room. When I made it to the front of the line, I sifted through the few that were left and grabbed my green notebook. It was identical to all the rest except for a white label in the left-hand corner with my name on it.

And except for a little piece of blue paper sticking out like a bookmark.

What?

My throat went totally dry and my heartbeat sped up. I didn't put a bookmark in my reader response journal when I used it a week ago. And I definitely didn't put in a blue bookmark that looked an awful lot like one of those mysterious notes.

I peered up at Ms. Sigafiss before removing the paper. Her back was still facing us since she was writing the questions on the board, which meant it was probably as safe as it was going to get. I took a deep breath as I tugged at the edges of the paper and opened it up.

Holy high heels.

There were teeny typed words on the paper, just like the last one. And my name was at the top.

Elyse,

If you want to feel better, introduce yourself to someone new, someone who you've never talked to before. I don't care who it is. I do care that you do it as soon as possible. If you get an interview, doing this will help you be more comfortable during the conversation!

I folded up the paper but then opened it again to make sure I had read it right and wasn't going bonkers. I scanned the room, not sure who or what I was looking for. No one looked back at me. I had just experienced something creepy and unexplainable for the third time—but to everyone else, nothing had changed.

I kinda wanted to tell Jeg, but I'd never be able to get to her with the Loud Crowd around her all the time. Plus, she probably wouldn't want to hear from me anyway, and I was still kinda mad at her, too. I could tell Nice Andy, but he'd probably want to tell Ms. Sigafiss or one of our other teachers or Mr. Todd. I could tell Mom, but she'd probably want to tell the police.

It's kind of weird how getting a mysterious note written especially for you can make you feel so alone.

I read the message again, and then I read it about a million more times until I could practically recite it by heart. Finally, I stuffed the paper in my pocket and tried to answer Ms. Sigafiss's questions in my reading journal, but it was no use. All I could do was think about how bad I wanted to take the note out again.

The idea of introducing myself to someone new was seriously scary. I wanted to know new people, but I wanted to magically know them without having to do the awkward first-conversation thing. Besides, it kinda seemed like all the girls from the two other elementary schools that had combined with ours wanted to be in the Loud Crowd. Any of them I went up to would laugh in my face.

Although, if this note-writer person really could help me be Explorer Leader, a little laugh in my face might be worth it in the long run. Without bothering to look down at my sleeves covering the words etched on my arms, I *knew* it would be worth it. I needed to be popular so I could get good names. And being Explorer Leader was the only way to make it happen. I had to get one of those interviews, and I had to knock it out of the park.

• • •

At lunchtime, I threw open the bathroom door and stopped dead in my tracks. Olivia was sitting on my bench.

For a minute, I just stared, a little annoyed. This was *my* secret spot, and the last thing I felt like doing was talking to someone. Or giving up the bench.

But then I remembered the note. **If you want to feel better, introduce yourself to someone new.** This would probably be the best chance I'd have. I guess it wouldn't kill me.

"Hey," Olivia said, looking at the book in my left

hand and the brown bag in my right. "Looks like we had the same idea."

"Yeah, I guess!" I gulped. I could do this. I talked to people all the time. And I also sometimes said my name. I could probably do the two together, if I stayed calm long enough to get the words out. "Um, I'm Elyse. We haven't really gotten to meet yet." *Hooray for me; I did it!*

"Yeah, hi!" Olivia scooted over a little to make room. She motioned toward the space next to her.

"Thanks." I sat down, and she smiled at me. "So . . . you like eating lunch in the bathroom?"

She laughed. "Yeah, sometimes. I haven't been doing it much, but I have to take quiet when I can get it. My house is always crazy."

"Oh yeah! You have a bunch of brothers and sisters, right?"

"Yeah! Do you have any?"

"Nope. If you ever get sick of yours, I'll borrow them."

Olivia laughed.

"How old are they?" I asked.

"Well . . ." She scratched her chin and laughed again. "I should know this. Okay, so Emmanuel is sixteen, and Vera is fourteen, and I'm eleven. Then Philip is eight, Farrah is five, and Matthew is two."

"Do you all get along?"

"Yeah . . . we don't have much choice. Farrah has

brittle-bone disease, so we all take care of her together. It's the mild kind, but still. I think we all feel kinda dumb about fighting when we think about what she has to deal with."

"Wow." Everything Olivia said made me want to be her friend even more. She really cared about people. And her sister—it might make me a little selfish, but the first thing I thought was that if Olivia was so kind to her sister, maybe she'd be kind to me, too, if she knew about my CAV.

But I couldn't bring myself to tell her. The second I considered it, my throat dried up so much that I couldn't say *anything*. So instead of talking, I smiled and opened up my book and my lunch. I grabbed my string cheese—courtesy of Nice Andy for the fifth day in a row (now his mom was buying extra for the middle school cheese-eaters)—and offered her a big chunk.

Olivia smiled and took it. Then she opened her book, too, and for the next twenty minutes we sat on our bench with our books, enjoying a little peace and quiet and cheese.

10
WALKS

ONE OF THE GOOD PARTS ABOUT BEING IN MIDDLE SCHOOL was that now I was allowed to go out by myself on the weekends as long as my homework was done and I promised to stay close. I could just decide, *Hey, I want to go for a walk,* and not have to wait around for Mom or Jeg or anyone to agree to go with me.

I didn't know where I was going when I started walking on Saturday morning. All I knew was that I was crunching in the leaves along the way, and the sun was out, and everything seemed perfect even though some things were a mess and I had lots of dumb, itchy words on my body to prove it. But I tried really hard not to let myself think about it—until I found myself at the big neighborhood field, right near the bleachers.

I looked around, like *How did I get here?* I didn't

mean to go to the field. I didn't want to be at the field. I'd rather have been at home, locked in my room with a thousand bottles of the thickest, goopiest, most disgusting anti-itch cream Mom could find than be at the field. Yet there I was. There, my feet had automatically taken me. Traitors.

Last year, Jeg and I had gone to the field all the time because we wanted fresh air, and also because we wanted to spy on Kevin and Liam. Mostly because we wanted to spy on Kevin and Liam.

They were on the soccer team that practiced every Saturday morning. We would pack bags of candy (for energy) and skip down the street, giggling the whole way because we would always say the same thing at the same time and it was hilarious. Everything was hilarious when I was with my best friend, even the stuff that wasn't really all that funny.

When we'd get to the field, we'd run and hide behind the rusty bleachers on the sidelines. If we sat criss-cross-applesauce, we were at the perfect angle where we could see out but people couldn't see in. From that position, we watched practice after practice, commenting the whole time about how cute Kevin looked in his uniform (Jeg) and how nice and focused Liam was (me).

"Everyone over here," a big voice boomed, snapping me out of my thoughts. People in blue jerseys poured in from all directions. I scrambled toward the bleachers and practically dove to my secret spot, getting a small grass stain on my jeans in the process. Whoops. Mom was not going to be too thrilled about that one.

"Morning! Let's run some drills," the same voice shouted. "Liam, you're up!"

Liam! I poked my head out, but he was hard to see. The soccer team had grown—there had to be at least twenty people out there—and they were all dressed in the same royal-blue-and-white uniform. They kept moving—ducking, weaving, tossing, turning, hokeying, pokeying, whatever else soccer players do—and right as I thought I saw Liam, he started running down the field in a different direction. Well, fine. I shouldn't want to see Liam anyway. I *didn't* want to, as a matter of fact. He'd dumped me, and that was that. It was really too bad that he happened to still be cute and funny and weird in the coolest way ever. I think all that stuff should automatically get taken away from you when you dump someone.

The one problem with Spying Saturdays was that Jeg and I had had to fully commit. Since the bleachers were at the far end of the field, we had to get there before the team did and then we couldn't leave until after they left, or else we'd risk being seen in the big open space between the bleachers and the street that led to my house.

As I sat under the bleachers now, I realized that I was extremely unprepared for this. I didn't have candy, for one thing. Or comfy pants. Or a friend. Also, I discovered, I really needed to go to the bathroom.

There was one at the end of the field I had come from, the side near my house, but no way was that going to happen. I'd basically have to run right through the middle of the game. I couldn't always tell which player Liam was, but he would have no trouble picking out the girl who wasn't supposed to be there.

"Great kick, Liam! Now pass it to Kevin so he can shoot." There was the coach's loud voice again.

I peered through the open space anxiously, hoping to somehow catch Liam's eye in the sea of soccer players. But what would be the point of that? His eye didn't want to see my eye, or else our eyes would still be going out, along with the rest of us. Him seeing me wouldn't magically remind him that he used to like me (and probably still could, if he tried hard enough).

I flapped my legs up and down in my criss-cross-applesauce position. Why did I have all that cocoa before I left for my walk? I should never, ever have two giant cups of cocoa—of anything, really—before I go on a walk. I had learned this lesson before. The tricky part was remembering not to be so dumb.

"AHHH!" **DUMB** formed on my leg, and I couldn't

help yelling out. That dumb word itched like crazy. I clasped my hands over my mouth.

Please don't let them have heard, I silently begged.

To my relief, there was no coach's voice booming, *Let's all go investigate that strange noise we just heard from the bleachers! It sounded like a girl being attacked by her own leg!* There was only the sound of kicking.

What was I going to do? They hadn't heard my *AHHH!*, but they would definitely hear the sound of a girl peeing behind a bleacher. And that was something I'd never do anyway.

If Jeg were here, she would come up with some brilliant plan that only Jeg would think of. It would be so much fun to pull off that I would forget that the whole reason for having it was that I was going to explode any second.

A few drops of water leaked from my eyes, so I looked up to force the tears back where they came from. I missed Jeg. I really did. And I missed Liam, and that made me feel like dirt. I had a new boyfriend, so I shouldn't miss my old one! But Nice Andy would never make me feel how Liam did, no matter how much string cheese he gave me. Liam was just the right amount of nice. He was a little weird, too. He *got* it. And he liked me. But then he changed his mind.

It seemed kinda stupid to miss people I saw every day. I mean, they were *right there.* But they weren't really them anymore. Jeg wasn't the Jeg I grew up with, and Liam wasn't acting like the Liam I went out with. It was like aliens had invaded their bodies or something. They looked the same (well, aside from Jeg's boring new hair), but they were not the same people.

And then I had a scary thought: *What if they weren't really the ones who had changed? What if it was me? What if I had been the one driving them away?*

Looking down at **DUMB** on my leg, it didn't seem like such a crazy idea.

The Explorer Leader would *never* drive people away. So many people would want to be the Explorer Leader's friend that the Explorer Leader wouldn't know what to do with them all.

If I were Explorer Leader, maybe even Liam would add some nice words to my poster. Maybe he'd want to be my friend for real. *Friend* wasn't as good as *boyfriend*, but it was better than nothing.

Now a few more tears crept out of my eyes and ran down my cheeks as I remembered how great it was having Liam like me. I tried to make myself focus on the soccer game, focus on the possibility of being Explorer Leader, focus on *something*, but instead I just teared up more. *Get it together, idiot!*

"EEK!" I yelped. **IDIOT** was like being attacked by a whole *swarm* of mosquitoes.

Stop calling yourself names! I yelled at myself in my brain using my loudest, angriest imaginary voice. *This has to stop! This is not helping, you . . . you . . . wonderful person, you!*

WONDERFUL PERSON formed right away, but it didn't feel good for more than a second. Then it turned scratchy, kind of like it knew, somehow, that it was a lie.

Finally, I couldn't hold it anymore. There was no getting around it: I had to go to the bathroom. Now. There was no way I'd ever make it home in time.

I stood up and tried to wipe the tears away with my sleeve, but I couldn't get them all. I needed more sleeves. Or fewer tears.

"Bring it in for a huddle," the coach yelled, and the players ran to the farthest corner of the field. This was my chance! I might have been an idiot who drove away best friends and boyfriends, but I was not going to be an idiot who drove away friends and boyfriends and also peed her pants.

I jumped out from behind the bleachers and practically flew across the field. I couldn't remember how long soccer huddles lasted, and I didn't really want to find out.

When I finally reached the bathroom, I grabbed the thick silver handle on the door and pushed with my whole body, but it didn't open. I pushed harder and harder. Nothing.

"Go, Sharks!" came a chorus of voices from behind me.

I pushed the door again and again and again. I rammed into it with my shoulder. I kicked it.

Please open, I pleaded. *I will never come back here again, I promise. I will stop thinking about Liam. I will stop missing Jeg. I will deal with Mom and Dad and everybody else. I will just keep going, somehow, if this door opens right now.*

But the dumb door still wouldn't open. I turned around, frantic. I didn't care who saw me freaking out. I needed a bathroom *now.*

"Hey, Elyse."

I sucked in my breath, terrified to turn around. I knew that snarky voice. *Why, world, why?*

"You, like, totes have to pull it. You're welcome." Her mean giggle echoed in my mind over and over again.

Maybe if I ran into the bathroom really super fast—and stayed there forever—Snotty Ami would forget I was here at all. She'd think she just imagined it. It was worth a try.

I pulled open the door, rushed in, did my thing, and waited. First I couldn't get to the bathroom fast enough; now I might never be able to leave. Why hadn't I just stayed home?

I counted to a thousand (or something sort of close, I hoped) and opened the door a crack. The coast *seemed* clear. I opened the door a little more, then a little more, and then slowly crept out.

"Oh, hey." Snotty Ami's voice made me jump. This time she faced me, like she had been hiding by the bathroom waiting for me to come out. Lindsey and Paige stood behind her—and so did Jeg. "Great idea to have us come here, Jeggie." Snotty Ami was talking to Jeg, but she was still looking at me, like it was more important that I heard her than Jeg did.

My eyes dropped from her face to something shiny on Snotty Ami's neck. She was wearing a silver necklace with a super-funky charm on it—a peace sign. I glanced at the rest of the Loud Crowd. They were all wearing similar ones that would probably fit together like a puzzle. I swallowed, hard. It was *our* Best Friends necklace—mine and Jeg's—but now it was in four parts. It was different. Cooler. Better.

And it wasn't ours anymore.

Snotty Ami saw me looking at it, and she twisted her mouth into a smug kind of smile.

"Jeggie's parents made those especially for us. Now that their jewelry line has blown up like *whoa* and they're even more famous than famous, it's, y'know, *kinda a big deal*."

My brain felt like it was a balloon someone had just popped, and now it was empty. I had nothing. So I scurried away without a word, hurrying past the soccer guys kicking balls into the goal, past the stupid bathroom with the stupid door you have to stupidly pull and not push, past the bleachers, past everything. As I fled, my arms and legs practically exploded with bad words. **LOSER. STUPID. UNLOVABLE. WORTHLESS. FREAK. GROSS. NOT GOOD ENOUGH.**

Stupid Liam! Stupid Jeg! *Stupid me!* I had never had bad words appear one after the next like this before those two messed everything up. They had not only ruined my life; they were also ruining my arms and legs. I hated them for it. At the same time, if one of them had wanted to hang out with me, I would have probably jumped at the chance. How weird was *that*? It just proved what I was already suspecting: the really messed-up one was me.

My limbs felt like one gigantic scratchy bodysuit. I scratched and scratched through my clothes, but none of the words felt any better. Getting home took a whole hour because I was too uncomfortable to walk the right way, and when I finally made it, Mom decided that I couldn't go out for walks by myself after all. It was just too risky.

11
DR. PATEL

AFTER MOM FINISHED SLATHERING ME WITH ANTI-ITCH cream and ran off to call Dr. Patel, I went straight to the bathroom and didn't come out for a long, long time. I hoped if I took a cold shower, it would make the words fade faster. Somehow that seemed pretty impossible, even if I scrubbed with Mom's fancy old-lady soap that could supposedly wash off ten years.

"Hurry up!" Mom pounded on the door. "Dr. Patel was able to squeeze us in. We need to go *now*."

I stood on my tiptoes on the bathroom rug. I had spontaneously decided to have a contest against myself to see how long I could stand like that before I fell down. Maybe it was babyish, but I didn't care. Sometimes you just feel like standing on your tiptoes (and avoiding the doctor) forever.

Thirty seconds! Thirty-one! Thirty-two! Thirty-three! I was the tiptoe-standing champion of the world! The imaginary crowd went wild! Thirty-four, thirty-five . . .

"Elyse, *now*! I mean it!" Mom called again, a little anger creeping into her voice this time.

How was I ever supposed to become the tiptoe-standing champion of the world when people kept interrupting me and making me do stuff I didn't want to do?

I tiptoed out of the bathroom. It still counted if I was moving, I decided. Thirty-six, thirty-seven . . . What do you even get if you set a world record anyway? A certificate? A medal? A million dollars? I bet Mom wouldn't be so annoyed if this experiment could get us a million bucks.

"Come on. I know you don't want to deal with this right now, but let's just get it over with." Mom stood by the garage door with her hands on her hips. She was already wearing her boring mom shoes, her boring mom jacket, and her boring mom hat. Jeg's mom had jackets made out of fake fur and purses decorated with sequins and rhinestones. My mom would never be like Jeg's mom if she kept making these terrible fashion decisions.

I tried nicely suggesting some adorable alternatives as

she opened the garage door and I tiptoed into the car. Thirty-eight, thirty-nine, forty!

"Have you ever thought about wearing more colors?" I asked. "Dark reds can be very nice this time of year. And some purple might bring out the green in your eyes."

"Where are you getting this?" Mom asked.

"*Gurly* magazine. And Jeg used to show me pictures from the fashion shows her parents had in Italy and Prague and New York, and you should have seen all the colors! You might also want to think about dyeing your hair. You're getting some grays."

"Can't imagine why," Mom mumbled, looking straight ahead. "Elyse, Jeg's mother may be more fashion-forward, but lately she's also been out of the country three hundred sixty-four days a year and makes her daughter stay here practically by herself so she can have a 'normal' life. Is that the kind of mother you'd like?"

I got the sense that this question had a right answer.

"No," I said. "I like my mother. I think she would look extra nice in colors, that's all." Silently, I added, *And maybe if you were cool, I'd be cool like Jeg. And she'd still be going to the field with me instead of the Loud Crowd.*

We drove the rest of the way to the doctor's office in

silence, listening to the soft hum of the car and the quiet music on the radio.

Mom was way overreacting. I may have had more words on me than ever before, and most—okay, all—of them were bad ones, but I would be fine. So it hadn't been my best day. Or week. Okay, year. *Whatever.* Dr. Patel was a nice guy, but I only ever saw him when I was itchy, it seemed like, and he wouldn't be able to make it any better. He never did.

"Let's go," she said, turning off the car. I didn't budge.

"Wouldn't you rather get a snack somewhere? I'm hungry."

"Elyse. We have an appointment."

"But I have an appointment with snacks. It's rude to keep them waiting."

"Now," Mom growled. I think she was getting a little sick of me. But if she hadn't gone and scheduled an annoying appointment without my permission, we wouldn't have had this problem in the first place.

Most people loved Dr. Patel's because his office looked like a toy store had thrown up. I had always thought it was a pretty bad plan, though. You give kids all these awesome toys for a few minutes, and then all of a sudden it's like, *Sorry, but you need to put the toys down now so we can do a lot of scary stuff to you and probably make you cry.* What kid wants to give up toys for that? What kid wants to give up toys at all? So then you end up with a bunch of sobbing, temper-tantrum-throwing children before they even go see the doctor.

Like I said, bad plan. *Duh,* doctors.

I didn't even bother working on the ten-thousand-piece jigsaw puzzle sitting on the huge round table while Mom talked to the receptionist and filled out some papers. I knew that getting one piece would make me want to get another piece, and there was no point in wanting to get a second piece. There wouldn't be time. There never was. Everybody treated it like such an emergency whenever I came here. It was never just an innocent checkup like the ones everybody else got. Instead of leaving with a sticker or a lollipop, I only left with the same problems I came with—and the feeling that I was nothing more than Dr. Patel's personal science project. All because of one dumb gene.

"You know, if we'd left when I wanted to leave, you'd have time to do a whole chunk of puzzle," Mom said as she plopped down on a fluffy teal cushion on the floor beside me.

That wasn't true and we both knew it.

"Elyse Everett?"

Mom and I got up and followed the nurse into Dr. Patel's office. The walls in this room were painted bright red, with other little decorations all over the place. You were supposed to think you were in a fire truck, which would be awesome if I were five. Okay, it was still awesome when I was eight, but I was drawing the line right here, at twelve. Fire trucks are dorky and that's all there is to it.

"So, Elyse, how have things been since the last time I saw you?" Dr. Patel came in and took a seat on a little rolling stool. "I heard from your mom that there was a little emergency today. Roll 'em up, please."

"No emergency. I'm fine." I rolled up my sleeves and pant legs.

Mom elbowed me.

"Ow. What? I'm fine!"

FINE popped up beneath my sock, near my ankle. It felt, well, *fine*.

"She's been doing okay overall," Mom said, "but I'm extremely concerned about the negative words we've been seeing lately. They seem worse than ever."

I started playing with the awesome—I mean, super-babyish—horn on Dr. Patel's desk as he glanced at my legs and jotted something down on his notepad.

"We're getting through it, though," Mom continued. "Sticks and stones . . ." Her voice trailed off.

Dr. Patel stopped writing so that he and Mom could both look at me like they felt really, really sorry for me.

It was pity. The word wasn't written on their faces, of course, but I knew that's what it was. They thought I was pitiful. I *was* pitiful.

"Yikes!" **PITIFUL** sprang up on my wrist right before both of their eyes.

Oh, no.

I looked back and forth from Mom to Dr. Patel and back again, but neither of them spoke.

"How did that happen?" Dr. Patel asked.

"You're the doctor," I said.

Mom gave me a look.

"What?" I raised my eyebrows. "He is! I don't know how it happened, I swear."

"Could it be possible . . . that you're calling yourself some of these names? In your mind?" When I didn't reply, Dr. Patel sighed. "Some of my colleagues have reported this in other cases around the world. I probably should have warned you about it, but I wasn't sure if or when it would happen—the age of onset ranges dramatically. We don't understand all of the details yet, but we're fairly certain that it can be a normal symptom for some people with CAV."

Well, super. My being "normal" made Mom look like she was going to cry any second.

"Have you had any other issues lately that I should know about?" Dr. Patel asked.

"Elyse has been wearing long pants and shirts with sleeves all the time," Mom said. "I thought it was just a phase, but—"

"It's been cold out!" I snapped.

"You started in June. It was cold then?"

I paused. It was kind of hard to argue that.

"She also went to a *meeting* not so long ago," Mom continued in a hushed voice, like the meeting was the disease, not CAV. "There was a competition we weren't expecting, and while she came in a very close second, she didn't win. And then this morning, she went for a walk. I don't know exactly what happened." She glanced at all the words that hadn't been there yesterday. "But I don't think it was the most fun she's ever had."

"People go to meetings," I said. "And take walks. It's not that crazy."

Dr. Patel scooted closer to get a better look at my words. **DUMB** was still there. So were **IDIOT**, **LOSER**, **STUPID**, **UNLOVABLE**, **WORTHLESS**, and **FREAK**, the whole crew. They were going in all different directions, and some were bigger than others, but they were all thick, dark, mean, and itchy, and felt like ridiculously scratchy clothes—the ones that also have ridiculously scratchy tags—I couldn't ever take off.

Mom had a lot of nerve not wanting to wear colors. Some of us didn't have a choice what color we wore.

Some of us had to wear black on our arms every single stupid day.

"This is a big change from when I saw you back in the spring at the end of the school year," Dr. Patel said. He picked up my left arm and dropped it in his. "You seemed really happy then, and you were in shorts and a T-shirt, if I recall correctly. Does this bother you?" He traced **STUPID** with his index finger.

"It just makes me want to scratch it," I said, jerking away.

Mom grabbed my hand and held it tightly so I couldn't actually scratch my arm. Well, that sure wasn't going to help anything.

"I'm sorry," Dr. Patel said, and I could tell by the way his eyes got big that he really was.

Still, when I blinked, tears stung my eyes. When you tell adults your problems, they're supposed to help you solve them. That's the way it works. Sometimes that was how it happened here, but usually one problem just led to more problems.

"You've got to try to cut back on the scratching. I know it's hard. But that doesn't seem to help your discomfort." He scooted his stool back.

"Elyse, sixth grade can be a tough time," Dr. Patel continued. "Things are changing. People are changing. Your body is changing."

Ew. I squirmed in my seat. That was one change we really did not need to discuss.

"Try to stay positive. I know it's hard. I'm going to advise that you use ice, extra-strength Tylenol, and maybe a little more prescription anti-itch cream than usual. Be sure to rest, too. And no heavy lifting or driving. But that shouldn't be too much of a problem yet." Dr. Patel smiled slightly. His eyes were still glued to that **UNLOVABLE** part of my wrist. "And maybe only call yourself nice names."

You think?

"It's too early for this," Mom said quietly.

"How is it too early? It's two o'clock." I glanced up at the clock that looked like a fire truck's tire.

"Too early in your life, I mean," she said to me, and then to Dr. Patel, "I'm afraid it's only going to get worse over time. Middle school and high school can be so socially and emotionally challenging. I'm worried for her."

Mom patted my leg, and I jerked it away as fast as I could. I wanted to turn the room into a real fire truck and hit the gas, speeding with the siren blaring so everyone would know to get out of my way.

"I understand your concern," Dr. Patel replied. "But whatever comes our way, we'll handle it together."

I looked back and forth between the two of them. So I was supposed to use ice and not drive. Fine. Done. As usual, this had been a waste of time. I could be up to, like, ten thousand seconds of standing on my tiptoes by now. I would never set any kind of record at this rate, except maybe a record for most annoying doctor appointments.

Mom said, "I think it would be nice for Elyse to have someone she could talk to who really understands what she's going through. Moving here so Elyse could see you was the best decision we ever made. But now that she's a little older, it'd be great for her to connect with someone about CAV besides her doctor, don't you think? Can she meet your other patient?"

My ears perked up. That actually *would* be kind of interesting. Dr. Patel had mentioned his other CAV patient every now and then, but "the other CAV patient" had always sounded like someone who wasn't quite real, like a ghost or a scarecrow or the imaginary rhinoceros friend I had when I was little. For some reason, I never really imagined the other CAV patient as a person just like me.

"I'd love to arrange that," Dr. Patel said. "Unfortunately, I can't do so without the patient's consent, and she has clearly stated multiple times that she wouldn't like to be contacted under any circumstances. I'm sorry."

"So it's a *she*!" I said. That narrowed it down a little. I could work with that.

"Yes." Dr. Patel laughed. "You got me there. But I'm afraid that's all I can share."

"I understand," Mom said. She turned to me and tucked a lock of my hair behind my ear. "Still want that snack?"

"Sure." If I couldn't have a new CAVvy best friend right this second, a snack would have to do.

• • •

I didn't forget about her, though. When I got home, I ran straight to my laptop and went to my online profile. I searched for groups with "CAV" in the title, and when that didn't get any results, I typed in "cognadjivisibilitis," and when that didn't work I typed in "words on body," but all I got in my results were groups for people who really, really, really love tattoos. So that probably wasn't it.

There had to be a way to find this person, whoever she was.

But she was nowhere to be found. Either she was super old and didn't know how to use a computer, or she really didn't want anyone to find her.

And none of the other CAV people around the world wanted anyone to find them, either.

A worried thought flickered across my mind—maybe all of these people were ashamed. Maybe they all walked around in their different parts of the world wearing long sleeves and long pants, even if they lived in hot places like Hawaii.

The thought made me feel more connected to the strangers than ever.

But it mostly just made me feel sad.

12
THE HALLWAY AND THE LIST

ON MONDAY, I DECIDED TO TAKE A QUICK LITTLE PEEK AT the Minnesota trip hallway, the one with all the posters. It didn't freak me out anymore; instead, it made me kind of excited. There was an energy there that you couldn't find in any other hallway of the school. Decorations were everywhere, and I could hear people buzzing with excitement in every direction I turned.

A few people I didn't know were gathered in front of a giant map of Minnesota plastered across the wall. Lots of landmarks were circled—Lake Superior, the Mall of America, Fort Snelling, a big zoo—everything anyone might ask about. There were photos next to the map, too. In one, a group of smiling kids stood in front of a log cabin with their arms around each other. Another one showed some girls on skis, waving their sticks in the air like champions. The third picture was a big group shot. Some guy in a furry hat was standing in front of a super-enthusiastic crowd. It looked like everyone was in the middle of clapping or cheering or both as the picture was being taken. Furry Hat Guy must be one of the past Explorer Leaders, I figured. He looked so happy.

Farther down from the pictures, there was a big piece of white construction paper mounted on the wall next to a couple of pens attached with thick tape. WHAT ARE YOU MOST LOOKING FORWARD TO ABOUT THE 6TH GRADE TRIP? the poster asked. A lot of people had already written on it.

Being away from my parents!!!

Hanging w/my gurlz ♡ ♡ ♡

Making new friends

Going skiing and sledding

No homework

I quickly grabbed one of the markers, looked around to make sure no one was watching, and added:

Being Explorer Leader!

I smiled to myself. Yeah, this trip would be fun. It would. Especially if I got the job.

• • •

At the end of the day, Mr. Todd made an announcement over the loudspeaker that the list had been posted in the main office. I'd never seen people want to go to the principal's office so bad. No one could get there fast enough. Of course, Snotty Ami got there first. I wasn't too far behind, but behind enough where I couldn't really see her. I could, however, hear her ear-breakingly loud squeal.

"I knew I'd be on the list," Snotty Ami told all of us unfortunate people stuck behind her. "I mean, since I won the super-important comp and all. I wasn't expecting the other people, though. Good luck," she snarled in my direction as I pushed my way forward. "You'll totes need it, dorkface."

I winced as **DORKFACE** sprang up on my shin.

"Don't worry, CAV girl," she said, winking as she pushed by me. "Your secret's safe with me."

I gulped as what she said sank in. Since the teachers hadn't threatened anyone about calling me names this year, and since Jeg and Liam weren't around to protect me anymore, what was to stop Snotty Ami—or anyone else—from calling me names? (Nothing would stop her, obviously. She had made that pretty clear.) And what would stop everyone from telling people from other elementary schools, like Olivia, that I had CAV?

Sure, Snotty Ami had said the secret was safe with her. But I trusted that about as much as I trusted that the tooth fairy was real.

But what had she meant by *Good luck*? It couldn't be that I—no, it couldn't. Unless . . .

As the crowd parted, I cautiously made my way up to the front with Nice Andy following behind.

EXPLORER LEADER INTERVIEWS

Elyse Everett (8:00 a.m. Tuesday)

JaShawn Talcott (8:30 a.m. Tuesday)

Ami Kowalski (11:00 a.m. Wednesday)

Andy Garvin (11:30 a.m. Wednesday)

Hector Ramirez (1:30 p.m. Thursday)

Layla Levine (2:00 p.m. Thursday)

"Did you see?" Nice Andy said.

"Uh, yeah!" I smiled so big that my face hurt. Forget Snotty Ami. I had a real chance at this.

"Sorry I have to totally destroy you!" Nice Andy said.

"We'll see about that." I glanced up at the clock. There wasn't much time between now and my interview, and I had major practicing to do. I said bye to Nice Andy and tore through the front office, propelled forward by **SPECIAL** and **IMPORTANT** forming on my arms. I got an interview! Now I just had to make sure Mr. Todd chose me for the decision that *really* counted.

13

PRISONER HORNS

THE NEXT MORNING AT 8:00 SHARP, I KNOCKED ON Mr. Todd's door.

"Elyse, come on in."

He smiled warmly while I tried to remember how to breathe. I followed him into his office and took a seat on his fluffy navy-blue couch. Principal Todd's personal motto was "If you're going to be blue, do it in style." He used to be a guidance counselor before he became a principal. Before that, I think he was probably a really wimpy kid. Lucky for him, he had grown up to look a lot like a grizzly bear.

"So you're here to interview for Explorer Leader for the sixth-grade Minnesota trip. You did a great job in the competition, and your grades and attendance are impeccable, but it's important for us to discuss the position in person, too. Why do you think you would do a good job?"

I want to be in charge of something. I want everybody to always say nice things to me. I want arms and legs that feel light and happy instead of itchy and annoying.

I don't even want it, really.

I need it.

But I didn't say that. Instead, I said, "Um, well, I'm really organized. I like planning. I'm good with details."

"I see. And do you have much experience being a leader? Or exploring?"

"Uh, I, er." My face grew hot and sticky. "I babysit my neighbors sometimes, which is a lot like being a leader, because I have to lead the kids to, uh, not do dangerous stuff." My hands were balled up, drenched in their own nasty hand sweat. What was this, an interview to become the president of the universe?

Mr. Todd glanced up from his notepad and looked me right in the eye. Holy high heels, he had eyeballs! That was a surprise considering he was such a furry guy. The eyeballs were on the smaller side, and the irises were a dark gray color I imagined all his mountains of hair would turn someday. Now if only I could find his nose.

"What would you do in an emergency out in the wilderness?"

"Ummmm," I said intelligently. *Think, bozo!*

BOZO sprang up near my elbow, and I yelped like a dog getting its tail stepped on. Itchy itchy itchy! *Don't scratch, don't scratch, don't scratch.*

I wanted to scratch *so* bad. But then Mr. Todd would see and would think about CAV instead of how I'd be a good Explorer Leader. And I bet he'd feel bad for me and **PITIFUL** would come back and the whole interview would just go from bad to worse.

So I really, really, *really* couldn't scratch.

Mr. Todd shot me a confused look. Every hair on his body looked at me like, *What's wrong with you?*

"I was just demonstrating," I said slowly, "how I would scream if there was an emergency out in the wilderness. So I could get help. Then I would probably call my mom." I flashed him a winning smile. Yes! Totally saved that one.

"Well, Elyse, I have no doubt that you'd plan the details to a T, but we need someone who can also take charge," Mr. Todd said hesitantly. "You know, someone who can grab the bull by the horns. Handle problems with a moment's notice. Take no prisoners. That kind of thing. Do you think you would be able to do that?"

My head bobbed up and down as I tried to stop the tears gathering at the sides of my eyes. "I can," I said. "I can grab the prisoners and take the horns." Wait, that wasn't how it went. Grab the horns and take the prisoners? Dumb Mr. Todd. Who talked like this, anyway, with all these metaphors and symbols and junk? Why couldn't he just say what he meant?

And why couldn't I?

"Thanks for coming in," he said as he got up to open the door. "I'm going to take some time to go over my notes and to gather recommendations and thoughts from teachers before announcing who goes on to the next round. It may take a few weeks or so. Remember, you're guaranteed a spot on the committee no matter what happens. You'll still have a lot of responsibility in planning our trip if that's where you end up."

I didn't want responsibility, though. Not really.

I wanted my face plastered on that question-mark poster in the hallway.

And I wanted the rest of that poster covered in compliments.

And now it didn't seem like any of that was going to happen.

"Thanks," I muttered as I lowered my head and scurried out the door, down the hall, and straight to my seat in Ms. Sigafiss's class. My legs throbbed thanks to the new additions of **TOTAL FAILURE** and **SUPER AWKWARD**. I couldn't believe how I'd managed to go from excited to miserable in the course of twenty minutes. Or how, for a second, I thought I actually had a chance at getting the best job in the world, the job that was clearly meant for someone like Snotty Ami and not someone like me. I was dumb to think that the job would make me cool. Apparently, to be seriously considered, you had to be cool already.

14
A REAL DATE

El,

I've made it to November! I'm trying really hard to size up the mystery-note-writer suspects, but I have no clue who it could be. Everyone seems innocent, but someone isn't. Maybe it's Olivia, trying to make friends with me in a sneaky way. But that doesn't make any sense, since she's so fun and bubbly and could be friends with anyone she wanted. She's the type of person who would just talk to me if she wanted to know me. Plus, the note writer knows I have CAV, and Olivia doesn't.

I hope.

(Does she know? Maybe you'll know by the

time you read this. If you don't, you should just ask her already, okay?)

I went over to her house yesterday after school, which was super weird just because it was Olivia's house and not Jeg's. It was fun, though. Her house was so cool. There was stuff everywhere, but you could tell it was because a big, happy family lived there, not because they were just a bunch of slobs. Her living room was like a museum, with pictures and school projects and really cool colorful masks hanging all over the walls.

"My parents collect African art," she said. "They think it keeps us connected to our heritage or something. I dunno. Parents, right?"

I smiled, still looking at the masks. They were unique. Part of the fun of going to someone's house for the first time is that you never know what new and interesting things you might see.

Maybe I'll start trying it some more, going to new people's houses. But also, more important, knowing new people.

And letting them know me.

Or maybe one is enough for now.

Olivia introduced me to her brothers and sisters (the ones who were home, anyway—she has so many!), and we ate cookies and had a dance party, with Farrah as the DJ. Olivia's room is pink, like mine, but she has pictures on the walls instead of posters. Pictures with her siblings, with her parents, a bazillion different friends from elementary school, from her camp, from everywhere.

Maybe I can be part of it someday. I hope so. (Maybe you're part of it by the time you read this! Are you?)

Unless, of course, Snotty Ami tells her about CAV before I do and ruins everything.

I can't tell her yet. I started to, but then Farrah turned the music up.

I probably could have tried again, but I didn't.

Yeah, so I chickened out. What about it?

Anyway, updated goals:

1. Remember that I like Nice Andy.
2. Convince Mr. Todd that I am perfectly capable of being the Explorer Leader.
3. Stop looking at Liam, and listening to him breathe, and being mad when he talks to girls who are not me.
4. Stop being weird (and calling myself weird, because now **WEIRD** has popped up **again** and

*it is really **not** a good time). Stop thinking, and focus on how I can get Explorer Leader!*

From,
November Self

• • •

I threw my notebook in my purse in the nick of time. Dad slammed on the brakes in front of the big Soup Palace sign, and I unbuckled my seat belt.

"So?" I asked, adjusting my long-sleeved light green sweater dress to make the sleeves go as far down as they could. Nice Andy obviously wouldn't care about my words, but you never knew about strangers. "How do I look?"

Dad's face froze. "Um . . . you look, uh, light green!"

I rolled my eyes. "Duh, Dad."

"Have fun," he said as I got out of the car, shut the door, and took a deep breath. I wasn't nervous, exactly, but I wasn't excited, either. "Love you."

"Love you. Bye." I went inside, where Nice Andy was waiting for me at the table closest to the door.

"Do you believe our parents let us go on a real date!"

"Uh, yeah, no. Pretty cool," I said. Only it wasn't pretty cool at all, or even a little cool. I had only agreed to it because he wanted to go to Soup Palace, and they have the best beef stew I've ever had in my entire life. Dad only agreed to it because Mom convinced him that it was just hanging out with a friend, plus she gave me extra money to bring home some amazing beef stew for him. He loved it almost as much as I did.

Nice Andy probably didn't need to know that.

"So what would you do if you had a million dollars?" Nice Andy asked after we had taken our soup back to our table, like it was a perfectly normal topic of conversation.

Buy a way out of this date, I said in my head. And all the beef stew I could eat. Out loud, I said, "I don't know. Give some to my mom and dad. Get some books. Maybe buy a candy store or two. Or"—my eyes grew wide—"buy a soup store! This soup store! Yes! Then I could have free beef stew anytime I wanted it."

He slurped his soup thoughtfully. I had never seen someone take such teeny spoonfuls before. We were going to be there until midnight, easily. I fidgeted in my seat.

"I think I'd get a time travel machine! Maybe see some history with my own eyes and try to help end wars and solve mysteries and stuff! And go back in time to relive the amazing day of my Explorer Leader interview!" He got a dreamy look in his eyes. "I can't believe Mr. Todd still hasn't told us who's going on to the next round! How long does it take to get recommendations from teachers?"

"I know. It's so annoying. Maybe he's waiting to announce it at the fund-raising show or something." I stared down into my almost-empty bowl. Was it time to go home yet? Things should end when I want them to end.

"Oh yeah! I bet he is! My interview was so awesome," he said, totally not picking up on my I-don't-want-to-talk-about-this vibe. "Mr. Todd said there were lots of great candidates! But he thought my responses were really enthusiastic! I don't know exactly what he meant by that, but I think it's a good sign!"

"Cool," I said. I thought about how excited he'd been after his interview, and how a teeny-tiny part of me had hoped his had gone badly, even worse than mine, just so I could know that that was possible. Even now, a couple of weeks later, the same mean thought was still nagging at me. I tried extra hard to push it away.

When I finally got Dad's text—Here! Hope you're having a SOUPER fun time in there!—I practically tripped over my feet and flew through the door because I was out of there so fast. I didn't even get Dad's soup.

"I'll text you!" Nice Andy yelled as I slammed the car door.

"Go, Dad, go!" I cried, like we were in a race or something.

Dad went.

"Was it fun?" he asked.

"It was . . . fun-ish," I said. "I don't know. I kinda wish it had been Olivia there instead of Andy."

Dad smiled. "I'm glad you've made a nice new friend." Then he started talking about the weather.

I closed my eyes, letting Dad's soft voice soothe me like a lullaby. I was happy that the night was over and I'd be home soon. Maybe Nice Andy would take the hint and be a little less annoying. I mean, if a girl is having a better time with her beef stew than she is with you, that has to tell you something.

Maybe he'd had a bad time, too. Maybe he was at his house right now thinking about how even though he liked my words, he didn't like me. I kinda hoped so.

But less than an hour after I walked in the door, there was his name attached to a new text on my phone:

i had so much fun with u. u are so awesome and cool! ☺ if u were an ice cream flavor what flavor would u be? ☺

What was so hard about leaving me alone? I would be leave-me-alone ice cream!

But then I looked at it again. He had called me awesome. And cool. I couldn't remember the last time someone had called me awesome and cool, let alone in the same sentence. And it felt pretty nice. It felt *really* nice, actually.

It was one thing for him to think CAV was cool and be way too nice to me about it. But if he wanted to be super-complimentary about it, well, he could go right ahead.

I responded:

Strawberry ☺

I put my phone away, just as **AWESOME** replaced **UNLOVABLE**, and **COOL** settled in right above **LOSER**, which was a little lighter than it had been yesterday. I moved my arm back and forth. It felt much better. In fact, my whole body did. Thanks to Nice Andy, this could possibly be a No-Cream Night for the first time in months!

Maybe he wasn't so bad after all. Plus, everyone knew that it was better to have a goofy boyfriend than no boyfriend at all. So I guess Nice Andy could stay.

15
THE SHOW

THE NEXT DAY IN ENGLISH, I SAID HI TO OLIVIA AND TOOK my seat. She wiggled her shoulders at me and giggled. It was one of the many so-bad-they're-good new dance moves we had invented at her house. Maybe the shoulder shake could be our secret greeting. I did it back to her, and it made me giggle so hard that I didn't notice Ms. Sigafiss staring at me from the front of the room.

"Elyse, I have a note for you," she said after a minute. "It was in my mailbox in the office this morning."

"Elyse, Teacher has a note for you!" Kevin repeated in a loud voice, causing everyone to burst into hysterics.

"I think she heard me the first time," Ms. Sigafiss said, glaring at him. "I'd be careful if I were you, Mr. Bata. I happen to know you've shown interest in being on the sixth-grade baseball team this spring. I would hate for that opportunity to be jeopardized."

While everyone looked at Kevin for his reaction, I looked at Jeg. This had to be a little distressing to her, seeing her boyfriend get threatened like that.

Sure enough, her face had concern scribbled all over it. I wanted to remind her that Kevin was really tough. He could handle things, and he'd never *actually* get in that much trouble from one little comment. But then I remembered that reminding Jeg about this kind of stuff was up to her new friends now, the friends she'd chosen over me.

So instead of looking at Jeg and trying to help her calm down with my mind, I looked at the piece of blue paper in my hand that Ms. Sigafiss had given me and began to unfold it. My gut knew what it was, but my brain couldn't believe it, even when I opened it and saw the familiar typed letters.

Elyse, ever thought about performing in the fund-raising show? It might get you one step closer to being Explorer Leader, but more important, wouldn't it be cool to hear everyone clapping for you up on stage? There's still a week left to sign up and two weeks until the show. Don't wait!

What the high heels? I opened my mouth, then closed it. I folded up the paper and stuffed it in my pocket. Nope. This one was just not gonna happen.

• • •

I realized too late that stuffing things in your pockets, if you're me, is a terrible idea considering how much Mom does laundry.

So I really shouldn't have been surprised when, the next night, she held up the crumpled piece of paper and asked all casually (like she hadn't been waiting to ask me this question the whole entire day), "What's this?"

Luckily the paper had ripped a little, so all she had was the part that said "performing in the fund-raising show" and not the part that was like "one step closer to being Explorer Leader." That whole thing would have been kinda hard to explain.

Of course, she insisted we go back to Dr. Patel's right away.

"I think it would be great for you to be in the show, sweetie," Mom told me in the car, "but I think we should just double-check that it's a good idea. You know, there have been a lot of bad words popping up lately, and that Explorer Leader contest didn't go as well as we would have liked. Maybe it would be smart to lie low for a while."

I glared at her. Wasn't she supposed to tell me I would do great and that worrying about it was silly?

But I knew, deep down, that worrying about it *wasn't* silly. It was real.

I was hoping that Mom might pretend it wasn't, though. That she'd pretend that I was a normal kid who could do normal things and have normal reactions if the things didn't go amazingly.

But we both knew I'd never be that kid.

16
THE ONLY CERTAIN THING

"IT'LL JUST BE A QUICK CHECK-IN, I PROMISE," MOM SAID for the thousandth time as we walked into Dr. Patel's office.

There was that ten-thousand-piece puzzle again, and again I was rushed into the firefighter room right away and there was no time to do it.

"Hello, ladies!" Dr. Patel said.

Hello, torture! I thought. The last thing I wanted to do was talk about everything that was wrong with me or had been wrong with me in the past or could be wrong with me in the future.

Mom started telling him the whole story right away, so I grabbed the fake fire-truck steering wheel (a new addition since my last visit!) and zoned out till she got to the end.

"And so, while I think it would be wonderful for Elyse to perform on the piano, I know how hard she can be on herself. And kids can be mean, and even a small mistake can become a really big deal. Just look at what's been going on with her for these past few weeks!" Mom grabbed my arms and pushed up my sleeves.

"Hey!" I jerked them back, but it was too late. Dr. Patel could see everything—**DUMB**, **WEIRD**, **AWESOME**, **COOL**—all of the words. I was a mix of happy and sad and itchy and not. My date with Nice Andy and the hangout with Olivia had helped, but not enough to make all the bad things go away. Jeg had still ditched me. Liam still didn't like me. I still wasn't Explorer Leader.

"You see?" Mom asked. "She's so easily influenced. This could take her back to when we saw you last—all bad stuff. Slathered in cream. Miserable."

I glanced at the fuzzy fire-dog puppet on Dr. Patel's desk and wondered if I got a say in any of this. Mom's worries made sense, I guess, but it would be nice to be asked what I thought, too. Even if I wasn't exactly sure what I thought.

"I see your concern completely," Dr. Patel said. "It's risky. The show could go badly, definitely. Not that I'm doubting your piano-playing skills or anything, Elyse." He flashed me a quick smile. "But it could also go really well. Get her more nice words, boost her confidence." He looked at me again. "The only certain thing in life is doubt. A performance might not go well. The floor of this office might crack open in the next minute and we could all fall through it."

"What does that have to do with anything?" I asked when I finally got to speak.

"I'm just saying, none of us know for sure what's going to happen. Ever. Anytime. With anything. So it comes down to how comfortable you are taking the risk. What's the worst thing that could happen?"

I considered it.

"I mess up. Bad. Everyone laughs and says horrible things about me. I think horrible things about me." In my head, I added, *And the mystery-note writer would be disappointed and probably wouldn't help me get Explorer Leader, the one thing that would cover me in good words from head to toe!*

"And if you mess up, bad, and everyone laughs and says horrible things, what would happen?" Dr. Patel asked. This seemed kind of silly. He already knew the answer, didn't he?

"Bad words would pop up on my arms and legs. They'd itch a lot. It'd be awful."

"But haven't bad words popped up before? And itched?"

"Yeah."

"And did you live?"

"I guess."

"So," Dr. Patel said, leaning back in his chair. "It's up to you. And I'll be here to help no matter what you decide. As your mom likes to say, sticks and stones . . ."

• • •

After a quick snack stop, we got home and I went straight over to my stash of piano books and flipped through them. There were some songs I knew really well. I had played them sort of recently when my grandparents came to visit.

Mom came over and sat next to me on the bench.

"So what do you think?" she asked.

I thought it was a bad idea. I thought it was basically asking for more bad words, more itchiness, more gunky goop. But at the same time, I had come this far with the mystery-note writer. I had followed all the instructions, done all the hard things, and survived. And if there was a chance—even a teeny tiny, barely there chance—that this person could get me Explorer Leader, well, I couldn't really quit now, could I? Especially since Mr. Todd had made it official on the morning announcements what Nice Andy and I already suspected—that at the show he'd be revealing who made the next round. He probably wouldn't pick someone who didn't bother to show up.

"I'm going to do it. I'll sign up tomorrow."

Mom's eyes welled up and she looked like she might cry. I couldn't tell if it would be a good cry or a bad cry. Maybe it was a scared cry. I felt a little like scared-crying myself.

17

AUDACITY

THE NIGHT OF THE SHOW, I WAS A NERVOUS WRECK. MY palms were so sweaty that I couldn't touch anything without leaving a disgusting liquid trail behind. My heart was lurchy like *whoa*, and it pounded so hard and so fast that I actually thought it was going to leap out of my body and do some laps around the room without me. And mixed with all of that was the terrible feeling that I was going to throw up or forget how to breathe or both at the same time.

"Hey," Dad said as we piled into the car. My hands were shaking so much that he had to open my door and put on my seat belt for me like I was a little kid. "At least the weather's nice tonight. Not a cloud in the sky. That's gotta be a good sign, right?"

Mom squeezed his shoulder.

"Elyse is going to be great," she said, more to Dad than to me.

He cleared his throat.

"Of course she is. No doubt in my mind. Who wants to listen to some smooth jazz?" He pushed the radio on.

"Are you okay, sweetie?" Mom asked.

"Sort of," I said, practically choking on my own spit. I couldn't even say two words without feeling like my whole body was going to collapse. I glanced down at my lucky gold-star socks. *You can do it,* they told me. But they were not very convincing.

"It's going to be good, sweetie," Mom said, reaching from the front seat to awkwardly grab my hand.

I held her hand for a second, but then I let go since I felt a little bad about getting my nasty, sweaty hand all over her clean mom hand. I guess she didn't care, though, because she reached for it again, and held it all the way until we got to school.

We paid, went in, and grabbed some spots near the middle of the crowd. I looked around for a friend, but Jeg was late (and I probably wouldn't sit with her anyway), and Olivia was sitting with all her siblings. Plus, a little tiny piece of me liked sitting close to a clean mom hand. Not that there was any way I was going to hold it at school or anything. But it was nice to know that it was there.

The auditorium had been decorated with signs. "Help us go to Minnesota!" one said in loopy writing. "Let's Explore More!" said another in small, nearly illegible writing. Another one asked in a bold green marker, "Who would be the best Explorer Leader?"

Me, I thought. I would do a great job. I would plan the trip perfectly, and it would be organized, exciting, and fun. And I might even plan things I knew other people would enjoy, like talking about silly stuff and doing boring things.

I would probably call them something else on the schedule, though.

Based on the interview with Mr. Todd, it felt like my chances weren't great. But if I could do this show—and the note writer saw me, somehow, and could change Mr. Todd's mind before he made his announcement—there was still hope.

All the posters with the past Explorer Leaders had been moved from the hallway into the auditorium. There was Cody again, and Jordan, and even more people from years and years and years ago. People from before I was alive. People from before color printing had been invented, even. People who were now famous, successful, and happy. And all because they got their start as Whitman Middle School's sixth-grade Explorer Leader. Each and every poster had compliments written around the pictures of the people, just like the ones I had already seen. To have a poster like that one day—with my picture and my compliments, to look back at forever and ever and ever—would be the best thing that could possibly happen.

Well, the best thing besides getting through this show without throwing up, that is.

The lights dimmed and my stomach did a thousand somersaults. Ms. Sigafiss went up on stage.

"As one of the sixth-grade teachers and the chair of the fund-raising show, I'd like to thank you all for coming tonight," she said. "With your support, our sixth graders will be able to go on a fully funded three-day excursion to Minnesota this winter. We are still looking for interested chaperones, so please contact Mr. Todd if you're available. Without further ado, here are the people you came to see: our wonderful, amazing sixth graders!" She smiled so wide I thought she was going to break her face.

I whispered to Mom, "She never smiles like that. She's really an evil genius."

Mom laughed. "Sure, honey."

"She is!"

Mom patted my leg. I was starting to get really sick of people patting my leg all the time.

Jeg finally showed up and went straight to the stage,

with Kevin following close behind. Jeg looked like she was ready to rock out while Kevin was dressed like he was going to play bingo with his grandparents. The crowd cheered like crazy.

"Summer lovin'," Jeg sang into the microphone, "had me a bla-ast!"

"Summer lovin'," Kevin sang, horribly off-key, "happened so fa-ast!" Kevin didn't seem to be bothered too much by the fact that he would never be a famous singer. He was laughing in between words, galloping in circles around Jeg, and doing crazy dance moves that didn't even come close to being actual dance moves. Jeg joined in, spinning in circles and finally ending the performance by jumping on Kevin's back. They struck a pose, and Jeg gave Kevin bunny ears behind his spiky black hair. The entire audience was hooting, even Dad.

I spotted Olivia in the crowd and we shared an eye roll and a shoulder shake. I don't know what show everyone else was watching, but whatever we had just seen was totally ridiculous. As I did a quick scan of the crowd, I noticed Liam in the very back row. He was looking at Kevin in the same I-want-to-be-you kind of way Jeg always looked at Snotty Ami.

"Those kids have major audacity," Dad whispered to me. I didn't know exactly what audacity was, but it sounded like something Dad thought I should get.

A few flute players took the stage, which, from the program, meant I was next. It was time to get up there. Dad threw an arm around me and squeezed me close, his eyes twinkling. "See you when you get back. Love you." It was pretty nice of him to say, I guess, but I couldn't shake the feeling that he didn't *really* know if I could do it. I didn't really know if I could do it, either.

I don't remember how I got to the stage. I was so nervous that I couldn't even feel my own body, couldn't feel my feet touching the floor, couldn't feel anything except for the butterflies in my stomach and the sweat drowning my hands. But somehow I got up to the front and I was there and my hands trembled and I thought they were going to fall right off my body and walk away, maybe go have ice cream. But they didn't.

I turned my attention away from the people, away from Ms. Sigafiss introducing me and Jeg staring blankly and Kevin whispering something to his friends and the Loud Crowd giggling and Nice Andy flashing me like ten thousand thumbs-up signs and Liam breathing and the lights going down and a hushed sound where people were quiet but they weren't really quiet because they were thinking about me in their minds, probably really bad, mean things, but it didn't matter because I was looking at the piano and the piano was looking at me and it said, *Chill, Elyse, chill and play, and only look at me, and play. And do it. Now.*

And I took a deep breath, and I did it.

I, Elyse Everett, did it.

And when it was over, people stood up and clapped and cheered and hooted and hollered. And by people I mean real-live people who weren't my parents. Actual people! Relief flowed through my entire body. I could breathe again. *I did this!*

"That was amazing!" Mom gushed as soon as I floated back to my seat next to her. "Honest to goodness, sweetie, that was the best I've ever heard you play that song." She had tears in her eyes. "My baby. I'm so, so, so proud of you. It was incredible." She hugged me until I was so squashed I was pretty much a human pancake.

Dad gave me a hug after Mom finally let go. "Nice job, kid." He opened his mouth like he was going to say something else, too, but he zipped it right back up. But I didn't need him to say anything, because I could already feel the words springing up under my clothes. **AMAZING. INCREDIBLE. BRAVE.** (That last one was from my own brain.)

It was the weirdest feeling, after that. The show continued, and I watched, but it was different from before. I was actually part of it now. I clapped and cheered, even for the Loud Crowd's dance. I smiled at people. I was here. I wasn't sure, but maybe this was audacity. It felt a lot like happy.

At the very end of the show, Mr. Todd went up on stage and thanked everyone again for coming. Then he paused and I took a huge deep breath, because I knew what was coming after that pause. The room went dead silent. He said, "I want to take this opportunity to also thank and congratulate every student who interviewed with me for the Explorer Leader role, and I appreciated your patience as I went over my notes and gathered teacher recommendations. I know whoever leads our trip will do a wonderful job. Unfortunately, there can be only one, and we still need to narrow the playing field a little more. I want to congratulate the following students, who are moving forward to the next round. Please come up on stage when you hear your name so we can all give you a round of applause . . ."

I held my breath.

"Ami, JaShawn, Andy, and . . ."

Please, please, please.

"Elyse."

YES!

Nice Andy and I high-fived on our way up. The whole crowd clapped for us like we had already won whatever competition was coming next. With the bright lights shining down on me and the applause booming in my ears, I almost forgot that Snotty Ami was on the stage with me, probably making some snotty face and thinking of names she wanted to call me.

"Final challenge, Explorer Leader hopefuls," Mr. Todd said with a giant grin. If principal-ing didn't work out, I was starting to think Mr. Todd might have a pretty solid future as a game show/reality TV host. "I'd like you each to create an activity you think would be fun for our trip. Write it out—in detail—and turn it in to me before winter break. May the best activity win. Thanks again for coming, all, and congratulations to our final four!"

I grinned into the audience, my brain already buzzing with ideas. Was the note writer out there? Had he or she seen my amazing performance? And seen how I'd made it to the final challenge? Maybe whoever it was actually knew what they were talking about, and now I really did have a chance at becoming Explorer Leader. At being a face on a poster that would be hung at fundraising shows for years to come. At being someone people would love and admire and continue to love and admire long after the Explorer Leader-ing was over.

And even the smallest chance at all of this happening was better than what I had before the show. I'd take it.

18

DOING

El!

What's up, lady? How's the future? I have to tell you, things have been looking up since the last time I wrote. Ever since the fund-raising show, I've been a doing dynamo. Something clicked, finally, and I actually did what I've been wanting to do—do! And now I'm sort of acting like a normal human being!

I hope when you read this you'll still be doing stuff, because I have a lot of lost time to make up for. Here are the goals:

1. Start doing more stuff.
2. Eat lunch with people in the cafeteria.

3. Try to actually like Nice Andy for other reasons besides the free beef stew and string cheese.
4. Make an amazing activity, and convince Mr. Todd that I would make an excellent Explorer Leader (though, no, I am not blue, and I do not want to sit on that stupid couch).
5. Find out who's writing me the blue notes—and why. Here's what I'm thinking at the moment:
   - It has to be someone who knows I have CAV, because of all the this-will-make-you-feel-better lines.
   - It has to be someone at school, because that's where I get all the notes.
   - It has to be someone who has a TON of blue paper.
   - None of these clues really narrow it down much at all.
   - Argh.

It must be so nice to be in the future. When you read this someday, you'll totally know who the note writer is, and probably the answers to all the other great mysteries of the universe, too. And don't worry about it or anything, but if you *don't know who wrote the notes, I, Elyse of the Past, will be* ***super*** *mad at you.*

No pressure.

From,
December Self

• • •

I closed my notebook, stuck it in my backpack, and took a huge deep breath.

"You can do this," I told my reflection in the bathroom mirror. In my long-sleeved black-and-white-striped shirt and red jeans, I actually didn't look too bad. You'd never know that there were all kinds of words hanging out under the cute clothes.

"You are having a good-hair day," I told myself. "You actually feel like talking to people for a little while. This. Is. The. Day."

I made my way out of the bathroom and down the hall. The cafeteria was busy. It made me both excited and scared to think that maybe the person writing me the notes would be in there with me. Who could it be? I couldn't stop thinking about it. A little part of me hoped it was Jeg or Liam. But it could be anybody. Nice Andy. Kevin. Lindsey. Snotty Ami, even. That wasn't super likely, but it wasn't impossible.

I couldn't help but notice some staring and whispering as I maneuvered my way through the crowds to get to Olivia's table. My heartbeat quickened. Snotty Ami or any other Loud Crowd members wouldn't have told people about CAV . . . Oh, who was I kidding? Of course they would.

So it was a major relief to spot Olivia and sit down with her, Nice Andy, and the Hannahs (Hannah Berkowitz and Hannah Zeller), who I don't know much about except that they had the same name, were best friends, and seemed really nice. And they totally were. After a few minutes, I forgot all about the whispers. We talked, we laughed, and we ate the chocolate chip cookies Nice Andy had baked specifically to thank me for going out with him this long. They were extremely delicious.

When I got up to grab another carton of chocolate milk (the thanks-for-going-out-with-me cookies required extra), I noticed a piece of blue paper on the ground by my table. I bent down to pick it up. This one was small—it was written on a Post-it instead of a regular piece of paper. But when I saw the letter *E* sticking out, I immediately knew that I was in for something.

Elyse,

Ready for your biggest challenge yet? You HAVE to do this one or else I won't help you *get Explorer Leader. You have to break up Jeg and Kevin ASAP. Or else no Explorer Leader. I mean it.*

What? I ran my hands through my hair and frowned. Something about this note was weirder than all the others. First of all, this one wasn't typed. It was written in plain old pencil by someone with handwriting even worse than my dad's, and his was really bad. Plus, this note didn't even mention the amazing activity I had to create and turn in to Mr. Todd to get Explorer Leader. And making me Explorer Leader was the whole point of the notes, wasn't it?

I slumped down in my seat, never taking my eyes off the paper in my hands. I couldn't do this one. There was no way. I knew what kind of person Jeg was deep down. Somewhere in there, under the mean giggles and the skinny jeans that were the same as the ones the rest of the Loud Crowd wore, she was the one who would be my bodyguard and have nacho-eating contests with me even though Mom would always say it wasn't a good idea. Breaking her and Kevin up would totally destroy her. I couldn't. I wouldn't. Even if she did kinda deserve it.

"You okay in there?" Olivia elbowed me.

"Yeah, sorry." I forced my eyes up and stuffed the paper in my pocket. This was a time for cookies and friends and milk and more cookies, not for freaking out.

Only maybe it was a time for freaking out after all, because only a second later, Jeg waltzed across the cafeteria arm in arm with Lindsey and Snotty Ami. She held a huge stack of something pink and sparkly. *Holy high heels.* My insides felt a little twisty as I realized that these were invitations to Jeg's annual birthday blowout.

Every year since we were little, Jeg had thrown a humongous birthday party. She'd invite all fifty kids in our grade and throw one of those unbelievable bashes like they showed in *Gurly* magazine. Her parties were the highlight of the year. Best friends got special privileges, too, like getting the second piece of cake and then getting to go eat it on your own personal horse or next to your own personal pop star. I wouldn't get to be the best friend this year, but darn it, I was still getting the cake.

I watched out of the corner of my eye as she gave invitations to Phoebe, Kevin, Elijah, Liam, Juliana, Naomi, Greta, Brady, Courtney, JaShawn, and Claire. Then she moved to another area and handed them to Layla, Kimberly, Lea, Brian, Hector, Gibson, Maya, Trynna, Mike, Curtis, Francheska, Riley, and Charlie. Jeg walked around the whole cafeteria until there were only four pink envelopes left in her hand.

She stopped in her tracks for a second and spun

around, clearly looking for specific people. *I'm over here,* I almost shouted, but I decided to let her come to me. I was pretty sure that was the polite thing to do. And I didn't *really* want to go up to her and her other friends anyway.

She smiled in my direction, and then bounced right over to our table.

"Hope you can come!" she squealed as she handed envelopes to Hannah, Hannah, Olivia, and Nice Andy.

And that was it. All the invitations were gone. She saw me looking at her empty hands and gave me one of those you-don't-get-it looks people give me when they pat my leg. Then she skipped away with Snotty Ami and Lindsey, laughing loudly at something (how was something *always* funny?), just as boppy and perky and annoying as she had come.

My friends all looked at me with shocked expressions.

Really? *Really?* I knew Jeg and I weren't best friends anymore, but it looked like everyone in sixth grade was invited to this party. Even Liam. Even Nice Andy. Everybody. My heart got lurchy again, but not in the excited/nervous way. More in the super-sad-and-trying-not-to-care-but-totally-failing kind of way.

"It's fine," I told all the concerned faces looking my way. "Seriously. No big deal."

And it wasn't. Mostly.

I felt around in my pocket, remembering the newest blue note. This one wasn't just a challenge. No, it was an opportunity. An opportunity not only to do something, but to make that something include revenge. I may not have had an invitation to the party, but I had another, different, more interesting type of invitation that was eagerly awaiting my RSVP.

• • •

When I got home from school, I went straight to my computer. I tried searching for CAV again, just for fun, but nothing came up. I clicked on Jeg's profile and saw that she had added pictures from last week, when she was apparently in France at a huge fashion show. You know, typical long weekend. I flipped through, and there was Jeg with fashion designers and models, then one of her with her parents, and then about a zillion more pictures with fashion designers and models. She really had the best life ever.

In one picture, a guy who looked around our age was kissing her cheek. He sorta looked like Kevin, with shiny, spiky black hair, but you could tell his Mohawk was a really, really expensive one, probably styled by Mr. Mohawk himself with designer gel. He was wearing a sparkly silver tie over a black button-down shirt, and as I looked closer, I saw that not one, but both of his ears had piercings. I wondered if Kevin had seen this—I was guessing not, because he usually had some kind of sports practice or club after school. Plus, his profile was pretty empty, so it seemed like he didn't really go online much at all. Maybe someone should bring this picture to his attention. Someone like me.

Mohawk Man—and Jeg—were going down. After all, the anonymous note writer wasn't the only person in the world who could write an anonymous note.

But how would I do it? I thought about it and thought about it, and just when I was about to give up, a stroke of genius flashed through my mind. Kevin might not go on too many different websites, but he probably checked his e-mail. I went to an e-mail site and created the most boring, could-be-anyone fake e-mail address it would let me make. Maybe it was a little devious, but I had to do what I had to do. And I had to do it. I opened up a new message, entered Kevin's e-mail address, and started to type.

Hey, have you seen the picture of Jeg and that guy with the Mohawk and the earrings? I heard from a lot of people that they kissed. And that they're still talking. I thought you should know.

My finger hovered over the send button above my message. Was I really going to do this? It was a pretty terrible thing to do. I hadn't heard that they kissed—him kissing her on the cheek in the picture didn't count—but it was totally possible. But was I a person who not only did regular things but also did bad things—things that would hurt someone I used to care about? And still did care about, even though she had become the clone of Snotty Ami?

But then I pictured Jeg's face as she gave out invitations to everyone at my table except me. And I decided that the answer was yes.

Only a few seconds later, I had a message back from Kevin, who didn't seem to mind that he didn't know who he was e-mailing.

> wow, sucks. i was actually gonna break up w/ her NEway cuz ever since the talent show she wants 2 do stuff 2gether all the time and its sooo annoying.

Whew! I smiled and deleted the fake account. So he was going to break up with her anyway. I guess that was good news, but I felt a little funny that I knew this before she did. And yet—mission accomplished.

19

UNFINISHED BUSINESS

I DIDN'T SLEEP AT ALL THAT NIGHT. I TOSSED AND TURNED, and when I did fall asleep, for about thirty seconds at the most, I had crazy dreams about Kevin and Jeg and Mohawk Man, whose Mohawk went from a regular Mohawk to a giant Mohawk, with like seventy-six angry spikes that kept poking me, hard. Then Mohawk Man's hair turned into bright-pink party invitations, and he kept waving them in my face, but I couldn't touch them no matter what I did. When I reached for one, I fell into a giant pit of crumpled blue papers that all had terrible words on them—words like **BAD FRIEND** and **JEALOUS FREAK.** When I woke up, the very same words were plastered across my legs. Itchy, itchy, itchy. I lay in bed for a good ten minutes before I got up, scratching and scratching and scratching the thick black letters. It was all so unfair. Why couldn't I just get zits like everybody else?

When I got to school, I was cranky, sleepy, and itchy, and my hair was doing things even weirder than a Mohawk that could grow seventy-six hot-pink sparkly spikes. It was *not* going to be a good day.

It was not going to be an easy day, either, I soon discovered. There was a blue note waiting for me first thing in English, stuck right to my seat. Oh. Boy.

Elyse,

Don't forget to turn in your activity idea before break! I'm sure you worked really hard on it. Feels good to try, doesn't it?

I turned the paper over, looking for more. I wasn't exactly sure what I wanted to see—maybe something like *Hey, thanks for following my instructions yesterday and breaking up Jeg and Kevin. You are a wonderful human being and will definitely get chosen for Explorer Leader.*

But there wasn't anything like that.

Weird.

I tucked the note in my pocket as Jeg came in and took her seat next to me. I felt her sadness without even looking at her. She looked at me for a split second before Snotty Ami scurried up to her.

"Jeggie, OMG, what's wrong?" Now the entire Loud

Crowd came over and formed a circle around her. There was a lot of noise, followed by a lot of sniffling and a lot of finger pointing in Kevin's direction. My mouth went dry with a throw-uppy kind of feeling, so I tried to make myself calm down. He was going to break up with her anyway, I reminded myself. Wait a second—*he was going to break up with her anyway!* There was no reason for me to be involved at all! It was already happening!

But maybe the note writer didn't know that, I thought. Maybe the note writer thought Kevin was as crazy about Jeg as she was about him. And then I thought, *Stop thinking! Don't risk thinking anything bad about yourself!* And so I started talking to Olivia instead. But thoughts of Kevin and Jeg and notes and Mohawks kept creeping into my mind and wouldn't go away.

That's the problem with things creeping into brains—once they're in there, you can't really get them out, even if you're a doing-person like me.

"Good morning," said Ms. Sigafiss. "Please turn to page thirty-nine of your books and read until I tell you to stop. We will not be talking during this time."

"But you're talking," said Kevin.

Ms. Sigafiss shot him a look.

I stifled a little laugh. Even Jeg giggled. My leg itched a little less. Maybe **JEALOUS FREAK** was fading. That'd be nice.

Before I let myself think about what I was doing, I wrote a note to Jeg and passed it very carefully to my right. *I heard about Kevin,* I wrote. *Sorry. I'm here for you if you need me.*

Jeg unfolded the paper and read it, and the corners of her mouth turned upward into the smallest of smiles. She took out her pen with the big purple flower at the end, scribbled something, and passed the note back.

At the same time Ms. Sigafiss stepped out of the room for a second, and of course everybody started talking at the top of their lungs. People mostly weren't having actual conversations; a lot of people were just like "Talk, talk, talkity talkity talk." Which was dumb. But also pretty hilarious.

I giggled along with everyone else, and then opened Jeg's note. *Thanks. Sorry I didn't invite you to my party. My friends didn't want me to. But you can come if you want.*

Woohoo! It didn't come in a sparkly pink envelope, but an invitation was still an invitation. And even though she was a popular snob and I had unnecessarily tried to break her up with her boyfriend for a gig I wasn't guaranteed to get, she was still my friend. Sorta.

Ms. Sigafiss came back in and a hush fell over the room.

"That's better," she said. "Now, what do you all need to be doing?"

I sighed as I buried my head back in my book. I couldn't wait to go to my other classes, where teachers actually did fun things with us. Ms. Sigafiss didn't seem to care about fun. All she cared about was making scary faces and keeping us quiet.

Quiet could be good, though. It gave me a chance to sneak another read of Jeg's note and squeal silently. *I'm going to the party! Amazing cake, look out!*

I snuck a few sheets of notebook paper into my book so it looked like I was reading, and quickly added a couple finishing touches to my activity idea. After watching a little too much Discovery Channel the other night (it was for research!), I thought it would be cool if we learned how to make a shelter in the wilderness using sticks, rope, tarps, and other explorer-y things. It seemed like something a lot of people would be interested in—including Mr. Todd. I made sure to note that the tarps could definitely be blue.

After class, I dropped off my idea in his office. I had worked really, really hard on this, and I hoped it showed. I went home with a smile on my face and a nervous thump in my heart. It was winter break, and it'd be filled with food, fun, family, friends, and a massive Jeg party at the end. Exciting things were happening, and even though they were scary, too, I felt ready to take on whatever came next.

20

PARTY PREP

THE NIGHT OF THE PARTY, MOM ASKED ME ABOUT TWELVE thousand million zillion times if I really, really, really wanted to go. I didn't know how else to tell her yes.

"I'm sure. Absolutely. Positively. *Sí, señora.*"

"But, honey, things have been so tense with Jeg. You haven't seen her once over break. Who are you going to hang out with?"

"Olivia. Or the Hannahs. Or Nice Andy. Or no one."

"But won't you feel a little uncomfortable there? I could give Dr. Patel a call and see what he says about it. Or maybe I could go with you for a little while, just until you get settled."

"Mo-om," I groaned. "I'm in sixth grade. Come on! Plus," I added, "the only certain thing in life is doubt. Sticks and stones. Hakuna matata. Hocus pocus. Et cetera."

Mom laughed. "Yes. Exactly. All of those things." She pulled me into a forceful hug. "It wouldn't be cool for me to come with you. I know. You're growing up so fast." She traced circles on my back with her fingers like she did whenever I couldn't sleep because I was itchy. Part of me wanted her to stop, but another part of me could stand there forever.

"I already slipped some maximum-strength cream into your purse," she added. "Just so you have it. In case."

I didn't say anything, but after a minute or two I looked up at her with pleading eyes. It was time for the hug to end so I could finish getting ready. And take the lotion out of my purse and put it in a top-secret hiding spot where she'd never find it. I was not going to be spending the night hiding in the bathroom slathering anti-itch goop all over myself, thank you very much.

Hopefully, there wouldn't be any major itches that needed gooping anyway.

Mom finally set me free, and I put the finishing touches on my outfit: a sparkly purple headband, dangly earrings, my classiest black-and-silver-striped socks, and shiny black boots. I considered adding my half-a-peace-sign necklace but left it on my dresser next to that lonely piece of gum.

I hadn't had a chance to throw that gum away yet, but I would.

"How do I look?" I asked Dad when we got in the car.

He quickly scanned me from head to toe and smiled. "You look, um, sparkly!" he said.

I sighed as **SPARKLY** formed on my leg. He was right. I *did* look sparkly. But was that really the best word he could come up with?

Luckily, Mom had more than enough good words to contribute.

"You look so beautiful," she said. "Very glamorous. Right, honey?" She elbowed Dad in the stomach and he jumped a little in his seat. **BEAUTIFUL** and **GLAMOROUS** popped up and felt good, but didn't do much to make all the butterflies in my stomach settle down.

"You've got to stop doing that while I'm driving!" he yelped. "It's not safe," he said to Mom in a quieter voice. Then he took a deep breath and his voice went back to normal. "But yes. Yes. You're right. About Elyse. And all of that."

"Greg," Mom said in the same kind of voice she used on me when I was in trouble. I wondered what Dad was in trouble for, but it was hard to pay attention to them. We had just passed the Ferris wheel at Navy Pier, so I knew we were only minutes away from downtown. I squirmed around in my seat. Couldn't Dad drive any faster?

A million zillion years later, we finally pulled up to

the hotel on Michigan Avenue. It was about a thousand stories high, and two humongous men in black suits stood in front of the door.

Mom turned around, smiled all big in a way that made me nervous, and asked, "Want me to walk in with you?"

I wanted to say *No way*, but the words wouldn't come out. There was no reason I needed to be nervous; I had been to tons of Jeg's parties just like this. And even though this time there would be closer to a hundred and fifty people (instead of just the regular fifty), it would be fine. And fun! But the noisy pounding in my heart didn't seem to agree.

"I can do it," I said in a shaky voice. I rubbed my arms and tried as hard as I could to remember the words that were under my sleeves. They were mostly good ones. *I* was mostly good. I could do this on my own. I could. I would.

I forced myself to get out of the car before I changed my mind.

"Bye," I called, waving.

But Mom and Dad didn't budge until I told my name to the Suit Guys and walked through the door. And even then it was hard to tell if they really left. But I kept moving, following the signs to the elevators and getting in. When the doors shut, I knew I was really, truly on my own.

For a second I thought about pressing 1 and going right back down to the ground floor. I imagined myself running past the Suit Guys and back into the car, which was probably still there, waiting for me to do just that.

And that was exactly why I couldn't.

21

JEG AROUND THE WORLD

THE ELEVATOR OPENED ON THE SEVENTY-FIFTH FLOOR, the one that said *Penthouse* next to it on the buttons. As soon as the doors opened, a huge sense of relief washed over me. This was just a Jeg party, and I would have friends here, and there would be *such good cake.* My mouth watered just thinking about it.

The hotel was decorated like fifty thousand other countries all at once, and they were all extremely fancy. A red carpet started right outside the elevator and continued for miles, it seemed like, twisting and turning in thousands of different directions. It had to be longer than the red carpets that actual celebrities had at their birthday parties. On my right, there were walls made out of glass, giving way to an incredible view. I could see the entire city, the lake, the TVs that were on in all the nearby buildings, and all the teeny people who were watching them. To my left, there were signs. "Jeg Around the World!" they announced in huge, sparkling letters.

I poked my head into each room I passed. They were all named for a different country. There was a taco/nacho bar in Mexico, henna tattoos in India, crepes in France, and clog dancing in Ireland. It was a typical Jeg party. Actually, it was a little less crazy than usual. I hadn't even seen any famous people yet.

I couldn't find Jeg or Olivia anywhere, but I did see pretty much everyone else in the entire school. They all passed in their little groups, and some of them gave me funny looks, but I didn't mind. I was busy Jegging around the world. Also looking for cake. Where in the world was the fancy cake?

I popped into China and opened a chocolate-covered fortune cookie. *Be wary of a tall stranger,* it said. Well, that was weird; I didn't know any tall strangers and I didn't plan on meeting any. But I would certainly eat the tasty cookie.

When I turned around to go to the next country, there was Liam, in the doorway, standing there like he was waiting for me.

I thought back to the fortune. Tall? Yes, he was. A stranger? Well, sort of. Even with the six magical days of going out we'd had, there was still a lot about him I didn't know, probably. He could be a stranger, sure. But I wasn't going to be wary. I was going to be awesome.

"Hey," he said.

A shiver zoomed down my spine from the sound of his voice.

"How's it going?"

"Great!" Calm down, self. That came out in a *way*-too-excited kind of voice.

"Cool."

He studied me, and I studied right back. There was a sparkle in his eyes that made me think he was figuring out the meaning of life, but maybe he was really figuring out more ways to make me nervous (if me being more nervous was even possible). Or maybe he was just thinking about French-fry pies. I might never know.

I hated how he looked at me with those dumb sparkly eyeballs of his. It was different from when anyone else looked at me. He wasn't just noticing my shirt or my hair or the teeny piece of fortune cookie that was probably stuck in my teeth, the things everyone else saw. It felt like he was trying to see right through me, trying to see the real person I was instead of the cool one I was trying to be.

"Stop," I said.

"Stop what?"

"Looking at me like that!"

"How am I looking at you?" He smirked like he already knew the answer.

"Cut it out!" *Holy high heels, did I really just say that?*

His lips relaxed into a thin smile.

"You've sure gotten sassy," he said.

Oh, hey, **SASSY**. That word didn't seem to know if it wanted to hurt me or help me. It just kinda made me jumpy.

"A lot of things have changed," I said, trying to make my voice stop wobbling. It was not the most cooperative.

"Yeah." He nodded. "You did great. Thanks."

I didn't know what he meant by that, but I was definitely going to take any compliments I could get, especially if he was the one giving them.

"You're welcome!"

We stood there looking at each other for what felt like hours. Liam didn't say anything more, but he didn't leave, either, or start talking to any of the other people who kept going in and out of the room.

I lingered, my heart thumping and making me feel like I was going to pass out any second, but in the very best possible way.

When he finally smiled one last time and wandered away, that feeling went away with him, all the way to

Israel. It was only down the hall, but still. I wanted it back *so bad.*

I sat down for a second to catch my breath. My heart was racing out of control. I glanced at my thin silver watch. Liam had talked to me for a whole four minutes! Maybe this had been his sneaky way of telling me he still liked me. Why would he talk to me for so long when there were so many people to hang out with and even more fun things to do and eat? Why did he give me that weird compliment that didn't make any sense? Why did he thank me, even though I had no clue what he was thanking me for? Maybe he was nervous. Maybe he *finally* liked me again!

I grinned like a total baboon. Maybe we could get back together! But first there was the pesky matter of breaking up with Nice Andy. Well, a girl had to do what a girl had to do. I could take care of it. Probably.

I sprinted out of the room and into the next one.

"G'day, Mates!" a giant green sign announced. Oh, how nice. I had run right into Australia, where Olivia was posing for a picture with a blow-up kangaroo.

"Guess what." I grabbed her arm once she'd passed the kangaroo to the next person in line. "It's not official, but I think Liam and I are going to get back together. Don't tell."

"That's so exciting!" she said. "What happened?"

"I don't know. We were talking for a little while. I got a feeling."

"That is so great!" she squealed. We held hands and jumped up and down a few times. (Okay, a hundred times. Whatever.) We sounded just like the Loud Crowd, but I was way too excited to care.

"Want to go surfing?" Olivia asked, looking toward a corner of the room where several surfboards were set up against a green screen. Someone was filming your rides and then editing the video to make it look like you were really surfing in the ocean. I was kind of surprised that Jeg's parents hadn't arranged to move an actual ocean to Chicago especially for the party.

"Yes, I do," I said, and off we went.

"Surfin' USA!" Olivia sang as she surfed.

I joined in.

"Surfin' USA!" Neither of us knew the rest of the words to the song, so we kept repeating those two over and over again until we were laughing too hard to sing.

When our turns were done, we wandered out of Australia.

"Where should we go next?" Olivia consulted her map of the two floors where the party was. It listed each country along with its room number and activities.

"Don't think about it," I told her, snatching the map out of her hands and crumpling it up to make a point.

"Let's just go . . ." I looked around. "That way!" I pointed down the stairs to my right. "Come on! Surfin' USA!" I encouraged. Surfin' USA had nothing to do with taking the stairs to the right. It didn't matter.

"Okay!" Olivia laughed. "Surfin' USA!"

"Wouldn't it technically be Surfin' Australia?" I asked as we ambled down the stairs to the next floor.

"I don't know," she said. "Don't think about it."

I smiled. And I didn't.

Downstairs, the party was totally raging. A DJ was hanging out in Holland, one of the hotel's huge conference rooms. Before we went in there, Olivia and I learned a cool soccer ball trick in Brazil, made our own anime characters in Japan, looked at some fancy art in Italy, and ate some awesome cheese and chocolate in Switzerland. Then we ran to the dance floor. I couldn't believe how much stuff I was doing, and without thinking one bit! Could it be that I was actually having *fun* at a party without my old best friend or my own personal pop star?

Just as we were getting our groove going, the music slowed down.

"Time to find someone special," the DJ crooned. No! I didn't want to find someone special. I wanted to keep dancing! Unless Liam was around . . .

The crowd thinned out, and Nice Andy came toward me from far away, almost in slow motion. *Don't think about it,* I told myself. Just do things. Be nice and dance with Nice Andy! He bought you soup. He called you awesome. He made you pictures after all the class CAV chats. You owe him!

As he came closer, though, it occurred to me that, *ew*, no way did I want to dance with Nice Andy. Even if he gave me all the beef stew, string cheese, and pictures in the world, he would still have spit bubbles at the corners of his mouth and a goofy, toothy grin and hands even sweatier than mine. The second my eyes spotted the shiny red exit sign, I knew I had to make a run for it. When Nice Andy turned his head for a second, I bolted, and I didn't stop running until I had safely reached Antarctica across the hall.

So maybe this wouldn't be the night of my first slow dance. It should be with Liam, anyway, I told myself, and squealed a little in my brain. We were *sooo* getting back together!

Olivia caught up to me and dragged me two rooms down, to Jamaica, otherwise known as the hotel's ginormous indoor pool. It was dark, but strings of multicolored lights strung all over made it seem like a bright paradise. Except it was really still a pool. I froze.

"Let's go swimming!" Olivia said as she glanced over at the complimentary bathing-suit shop set up by the locker rooms. Most people had brought their own suits, but Jeg had probably figured that some people would forget and she wouldn't want anyone to miss any swimming fun.

I let out a quiet groan. I was one of the people who forgot, except actually I hadn't brought a suit on purpose. Wearing a swimsuit meant showing my word-covered arms and legs to Olivia for the first time. Maybe she already knew, but she had never said anything, so maybe she didn't know. And while my words were mostly cool at the moment, it was still a big deal to explain the whole thing to people who didn't know about it. Not to mention, I'd be reminding all the people in my grade who had forgotten or stopped caring. But since I was all about doing stuff now instead of thinking, did that mean I had to grab one of the freebie suits and swim? I didn't want to do it. Even though the water looked all warm and sparkly and I was still a little bit chilly from my minute in Antarctica.

My phone buzzed with a text from Dad.

Will be there soon. They say you spend six months of your life waiting for red lights to change. I am well on my way. Hope you're having fun!

I didn't totally want to leave, but I didn't totally want to stay, either. I knew that this was probably the best opportunity I'd have to make my exit.

"I actually have to go," I told Olivia in a voice that I tried to make sound really sad. "My dad's coming. Boo! I really wanted to swim." Not.

I sprinted out of the pool area in record time and hopped into the elevator. *I would have gone swimming if I'd had time,* I told myself as the elevator took me to the ground floor. *Even if that meant Olivia would see my words. I would have. Dumb Dad had to come and interrupt.* Still, I smiled. Except for a few little details, the night had been totally perfect.

I ran into Jeg's mom on my way out.

"Hey, girlfriend! How are ya?" She kissed both of my cheeks.

"Good." I smiled up at her. Wow. She had grown like another five inches since I'd see her last—actually, that was just her shoes. Holy high heels, how did she walk in those things? Or even stand? Other than that, she looked the same as always. Her long, wavy black hair fell all the way to her hips. Her makeup was perfect, down to her dark purple lips and silver sparkles clinging to her eyelashes. It must have taken her, like, more years to get ready than I'd been alive.

"Your outfit is adorbs, *dahling*. You are just fab. Kisses!" She took a sip of her drink and looked away, so I guess the conversation was over. I should have been annoyed—Jeg's mom talked a lot like Snotty Ami, after all—but I was too excited from the awesomeness of the night. Anyway, if you're all fancy and famous, you can probably get away with talking however you want. And **FAB** and **ADORBS** were very new and interesting words to have on my body.

"How'd it go?" Dad asked when I got in the car. I slunk down in the front seat and leaned against my seat belt. It was just hitting me that I was completely exhausted.

But happy. Adorbs. Fab. Probably getting back together with Liam.

Holy high heels. Liam. I felt my face getting hot and red. This was probably not a Dad kind of conversation. I'd try to talk about things he was interested in instead.

"It was good. Weather's not too bad tonight, huh? Did you make it through all the red lights?"

As if right on cue, the yellow light in front of us turned red and we stopped. Dad looked over in my direction. He was smiling, but he had big, sad eyes. What did he have to be sad about?

"Yeah, I made it through the red lights. Except this one." He laughed awkwardly. "Ha, ha, ha."

The conversation came to a quick end after that. I leaned back in my seat and closed my eyes, pretending that the hum of the car and the peaceful night had rocked me right to sleep.

And then we were home. Dad gently jostled me "awake," and I got into my own bed and actually went to sleep and had very nice dreams of Liam and me getting back together and being weird together and traveling across the world. It was only when I woke up in the morning that I realized I had never gotten any cake.

22
A PROJECT

BY MONDAY MORNING, NOT GETTING ANY CAKE WAS THE least of my worries.

The first day back after winter break is always the worst thing ever. But on this Monday, not only did I wake up with the super-bummed ugh-I-have-to-wake-up-early-and-go-to-school feeling, I woke up with a funny feeling, too. Something felt *off,* like it had that day when Liam broke up with me. When I got to school, I noticed Jeg bouncing in, wearing about a dozen jangly beaded bracelets, her dumb one-fourth-of-a-peace-sign necklace, and an enormous smile on her face. She was probably just happy that she'd had a good party.

Really happy.

But then Liam came in with a big smile, too. And

then they looked at each other, still grinning all goofy, and then Liam grabbed Jeg's hand and held it all the way to her seat, where he let it go, then kept grinning stupidly all the way to his seat on the way other side of the room.

I really thought I was going to throw up, but somehow I didn't. Which was very lucky, because I'd had rainbow sprinkles on my pancakes for breakfast and it would've been a very colorful, very embarrassing kind of vomit.

The room started buzzing, but I couldn't hear or see or think. I couldn't do anything. I overheard little bits and pieces. "Going out!" "Since the party!" "He's liked her forever!" "So cool!" "Great couple!"

My face grew hotter and hotter. How could this happen? Liam was supposed to be getting back together with me, not going out with her! And she was supposed to be someone who sort of cared how I felt about things like that! Why had she invited me to her party if she didn't?

I couldn't look at either one of them for the rest of the day. I sat in the bathroom at lunch with my book because I couldn't possibly face the two of them, all happy and stuff, parading around like they were the king and queen of England, and I didn't want to talk to anyone else, either. I especially didn't want to talk to

Nice Andy and stare into his nice face and watch him eat his nice food and nicely tell me how cool and awesome I am even after I had abandoned him in Amsterdam. How cool and awesome could I possibly be if Liam would rather go out with Jeg than me? Even Mr. Todd's announcement over the loudspeaker that he'd be making the Explorer Leader decision this week couldn't cheer me up.

• • •

By nighttime, my face had changed from sort of getting gross to totally puffy and full of nasty I've-been-crying-forever eyeball gunk. Disgusting. Like even more disgusting than disgusting. Like, disgusting-looking people would be embarrassed if they saw me. They'd be disgusted, in fact.

DISGUSTING settled on my arm and made itself comfortable (and me miserable). Mom stuck my hands in oven mitts so I wouldn't scratch and made me look at a zillion old pictures with her as a distraction. All it did was remind me that I'm older than I used to be and I should be having an awesome pre-teenagery life but instead I'm stuck spending my nights with my hands in oven mitts.

Seeing myself looking happy should have made me

happy, but it didn't. We looked at this whole photo album filled with pictures from my cupcake-themed ninth birthday party, which we'd had at a bakery. Everyone was dressed up. I'm in a sleeveless pink-and-purple-striped dress. My arms are draped around Jeg in picture after picture after picture, so you can't see all the words on me, but you can see **AWESOME**, **FUN**, **FUNNY**, **COOL**, and the one I loved the most, **FANTABULOUS**. Jeg used to call me fantabulous all the time. In our world, it was the biggest compliment you could get. No one even cared how many compliments were on me, though. Or how many not-so-great words. They weren't a big deal to any of us, not even to me. They were just there, like our birthmarks and freckles.

That birthday party was so fun. I mean, it was no Jeg party, but I had all my friends and all the cupcakes we could eat, and I was happy.

I kinda thought it would always be like that. Seeing the pictures just made me remember that that's another thing I was wrong about.

It's so weird, how one day you can feel on top of the world, and the next, that same world is crashing down in your face.

After Mom went to bed, I got up and went over to my desk. It seemed like as good a time as any to write my monthly letter to myself.

El,

Please tell me you're reading this. I need to know that you survived, that you're done with **DISGUSTING**, and maybe that the whole thing was a terrible dream because there's no way Jeg and Liam would ever really go out with each other.

All of this doing stuff has been for nothing, basically. Doing stuff has been a good distraction from thinking, but it hasn't really made my life better, and it hasn't made me Explorer Leader yet. And it hasn't stopped bad things from creeping into my brain and coming out on my body. So. I guess that's that, then.

Goals:

- None. Why bother?

From,
January Girl

• • •

I put my notebook back on my desk, and that's when I saw it.

In my *house.*

Well, technically it was peeking out of the smallest zipper compartment of my backpack. But my backpack was in my house. In my room. Hanging off my desk chair.

Which meant that someone had been *in my backpack*.

How was this possible? And when and where had it happened?

But, of course, there was a more urgent question on my mind: What the heck was this blue note going to say?

Elyse,

"There is nothing either good or bad but thinking makes it so."

(I can't take credit for that. Shakespeare came up with it. Pretty smart guy, wasn't he?)

For whatever reason, today was hard for you, but try not to think anything bad about yourself. Just be.

Tomorrow will be better.

Hmm. I folded the paper up and zipped it safely into the compartment it came from.

That was surprisingly nice of my mystery person. No tough jobs today, just some friendly advice. Despite everything, it was good to know that there was one person still in my corner.

• • •

I tugged at my sleeves, pulling them all the way down so my thumbs fit through the holes designed specifically for them. For some reason, there were always more words on my arms during the winter, so many that my arms didn't have room for them and they'd travel down to my hands. Mittens looked a little awkward indoors, but crazy long-sleeved shirts didn't. In fact, they were sort of stylish this season, according to *Gurly* magazine. So that was a relief. I glanced over at the puzzle in the waiting room. Maybe, if I went over there and worked really fast—

"Elyse Everett?"

Darn.

Mom and I dashed into the office and got settled in our usual chairs as Dr. Patel came in.

"How's it going today?" He smiled.

Mom and I exchanged a look.

"Not great," I said. "Shocker, right?"

He raised his eyebrows. "Show me."

I pushed up my pants and my sleeves. There were a couple of good words still there from my quick chat with Jeg's mom, but they had mostly faded and you had to squint really hard to see them. The bad words were the boss again.

"Hmm." Dr. Patel scratched his beard. "So last time you were here, you were contemplating whether to participate in that talent show. I take it that didn't go well?"

"No, it did!" Mom said. "She performed wonderfully."

"Yeah," I agreed. "I did."

"Great to hear," he said. "Then what's going on with all of this?"

I looked down at my shoes. I didn't really want to explain to my old guy doctor that this was all because of a boy and a bad friend. So embarrassing.

"There've been some social struggles," Mom said like she was an expert on everything that was happening. I did my very best to be nice and not roll my eyes.

"Hmm," Dr. Patel said again, looking me up and down. "And all of these negative words, have they been from the mouths of others? Or from up here?" He tapped on his forehead with his pen.

"Um . . . they might be from that area. Mostly."

He and Mom both looked at me like they felt sorry for me, and I wished that I could disappear right then and there. Those looks weren't making anything better, that was for sure.

"Maybe if you focus on something else," Dr. Patel suggested. "A project of some kind. Something to take your mind off whatever issues you're having with your friends."

"You still don't know for sure about Explorer Leader," Mom added. "It's a very special honor at her school," she told Dr. Patel. "She finds out sometime this week. And if you don't get it, Elyse, you'll be on the committee. You'll still be an important helper. I really think you'll get the job, though, despite how you doubt yourself so much."

"I don't know," I mumbled. "I don't think Mr. Todd thinks I'm the best person for it." It was true. He didn't think I could grab the horns on the bull or however that saying went. He told me himself.

But, I remembered, there was still the hope that my activity—or the note writer or both—could change Mr. Todd's mind. Yeah. And then I'd be the most popular person in sixth grade, and I'd feel amazing, too.

I smiled a little. That could really happen. It could all work out dandier than a dandelion.

"I guess I don't know for sure," I added. "It could be me. And if it's not, being on the committee would be cool, too."

They both nodded and smiled at me like I was such a good little girl for agreeing with them. But I had something else in mind, a slightly different, better kind of project that was slowly becoming an actual plan.

I was finally going to do something to figure out who wrote the notes, and get him or her to hurry the high heels up and talk to Mr. Todd. And I was going to do it soon.

"Great appointment, guys," I said, pushing my sleeves and pant legs down. "Ready to go, Mom?"

"I guess so. Unless there's any additional information we need or any new developments you want to tell us about—creams, advances, anything . . ."

Dr. Patel shook his head. "Not today, I'm afraid."

I looked him right in the eye. "But maybe another day?"

He patted my leg. "Maybe another day," he said. "Maybe another day."

23

CRAZY BOMBS

I WALKED INTO SCHOOL THE NEXT DAY WITH A MISSION. Instead of grabbing my books from my locker and heading straight to class like normal, I made sure to keep an eye out for suspicious activity. I scoured the floor for blue papers and peered into every eyeball, looking for ones that seemed guilty. But this was only part one.

When I finally made it to class, I was quick to take my notebooks and pencils out and pull my sleeves down as far as humanly possible so that no one could see **WORTHLESS** and **TOTAL LOSER** on my wrists. Then I got down to business. Maybe the note writer was someone in this class—but no one was writing on blue paper. This was going to be harder than I thought.

"Elyse, Mr. Todd wants to see you," Ms. Sigafiss said.

Everyone went "Oooooh" and turned around to look

at me, and I knew my face had turned the color of a strawberry.

I gathered all my stuff, dropping like five hundred things in the process, and I didn't even have five hundred things with me.

"Oooooh," everyone went again. Awesome.

KLUTZ bumped onto my right elbow and pinched me like a bug bite. If only there was a special bug spray I could wear to protect me from these words.

I scurried out of the room, down the hall, and into Mr. Todd's office. I nearly collapsed on the blue couch, tired from being pinched and tired in general.

But also a little excited. Was this the moment I had been waiting for?

"Feeling blue?" he asked in a quiet voice.

"No," I said.

LIAR. Ugh.

He eyed me suspiciously, like he could see the word through my sleeve and knew how badly I wanted to scratch it. Didn't he have any important principal-ing things to tend to? There had to be some kid doing something bad somewhere in the building, but here he was, trying to get *me* to admit I felt blue.

"Well, even if you *are* feeling blue, or even blue-ish"—he eyed me again—"I think I have some news that's going to brighten your day."

Now I was interested. Very interested. I sat up straight, showing him just how non-blue I was. Blue people were usually slouchy people, after all.

"I've noticed that lately you've been a little more . . ." He paused, leaning back in his big black chair and scratching his hairy chin. "Proactive than usual. I was really impressed with your performance in the fund-raising show, and it seems that since then, you've been extremely engaged socially with your peers and with the greater community."

"Yeah," I said. "It's nice that someone noticed!"

"I was also extremely impressed by the activity idea you turned in. It was thorough, well-researched, and relevant to the type of trip we're trying to plan. With all of this in mind, I can tell that you want to be Explorer Leader, and I think you'd be a very good one."

I could hardly believe what I was hearing.

"Wait." I leaned forward, almost falling off the blue couch. Such a klutz. My face felt red, but in a super-duper, crazy-happy-excited kind of way. "Are you serious? You want to make *me* the Explorer Leader? Me, Elyse Everett. *Really?*"

He smiled. "Is that a problem?"

"No! No!" Now I *had* fallen off the couch. **KLUTZ** got bigger and itchier, but I was more focused on the amazing sensation of **WINNER** growing on my left knee.

"That is so not a problem. I can do that. I can definitely do that."

"Glad to hear it." He got up. "I'll be in touch about your responsibilities, but know that it's going to be a lot of work. I'm going to depend on you to plan activities and meals, but there's plenty of time for you and the committee to work together before February. Here are some things you might find helpful—a basic outline of the schedule, some articles on leadership, and useful e-mail addresses and phone numbers." He handed me a ginormous stack of papers. "Oh—and one more thing before you go. Look, I want you to know that I have a lot more hair than most people." He motioned to the furry arms that stuck out of his short-sleeved shirt. The Loud Crowd could make thousands of little French braids out of all that hair.

"Uh, that's nice."

What is a person supposed to say to that?

He looked at me like he was trying to tell me something really important, but it's hard to concentrate on important things when you want to squeal your brains out.

"It's not particularly nice, Elyse. It's often embarrassing. I *could* do something to remove it, but that would require a lot of time and energy. So instead, I'm okay with it. This is who I am. I'm a man who has more hair than most. So be it."

"Um, yes," I said, my heart racing because I really wanted to get out of there and go tell everyone my news. "So be it." I tapped my foot and bounced up and down in my seat. *Set me free, you hairy, hairy man!*

"Well," he said, staring at me with his teeny eyeballs. "I suppose that's it. We'll talk soon. Have a nice rest of your day."

I skipped out of his office all the way down the hall. I was going to be Explorer Leader! This was happening! It didn't even seem real, but it was. It really, really was. This was *my life*. My fabulous, wonderful life.

With each step I took, I felt happier and lighter as my awful words disappeared, then even more amazing as they were replaced with words like **COOL** and **AWESOME** and **BEST**. Only the coolest and most awesome and best person was picked for something like this. And I was that person! It was already having the effect I wanted, and no one else even knew about it yet, which meant it could only get better from here.

I walked slowly down the hall where the Explorer Leader posters had been placed after the show. The one with the giant question mark in the face wasn't a question anymore. It had an answer, and that answer was me. Me!

I opened Ms. Sigafiss's door slowly and tried to sneak back in without distracting people too much. But it was hard. I was about to burst. This was the kind of thing that needed to be shouted from the rooftops, or at least announced to the whole class.

"Do you want to tell us why Mr. Todd wanted to see you, Ms. Everett?"

Ms. Sigafiss's voice made me jump. I wasn't sure if it was because she was talking to me or if it was because she was actually using a nice, friendly voice when there weren't any parents in the room. It was almost too nice of a voice. Was this a trap? And how did she know I'd want to share what Mr. Todd told me?

Maybe he told the teachers before he told me. That must be it. But it didn't really matter, because here was my chance to shout it from the back of the classroom, and I was certainly not going to waste it.

"Um," I said, probably blushing as everyone's eyes turned toward me. "He told me that . . . that . . . I'm the Explorer Leader."

For a second the whole room went silent. I realized after I said it that some people might be mad. Snotty Ami, for one. And maybe even Nice Andy. They had both wanted it bad, too.

I was wrong about Nice Andy, of course. After the silence ended, he and Olivia leaped out of their chairs and gave me great big tackle hugs.

"Explorer Leader Elyse!" Kevin yelled, jumping out

of his chair and clapping like crazy. Soon a bunch of other people joined in, too. I laughed a little. People cared a lot more about making a scene than celebrating me, but it was still pretty cool. Really cool.

I glanced over at Jeg and Liam, and they were looking at each other—gross—but they were clapping, too. A big I-love-everybody feeling came over me, and I wanted to give everyone a huge hug, except for those two. Okay, and except for Snotty Ami and Paige and Lindsey and the rest of the Loud Crowd, and except for Ms. Sigafiss. But otherwise, everybody.

"Stop it!" Ms. Sigafiss shouted. The room was getting really loud and rowdy. "Stop it right now. This level of noise is unacceptable."

"Yeah, stop it," Snotty Ami echoed as the room quieted down a little. "It's totes not a big deal."

"Jealous, much?" Nice Andy retorted.

"No." Snotty Ami stood up. "But just because Elyse has CA—"

"Cavities," I quickly jumped in. I knew I couldn't hide CAV forever, and most people probably knew anyway, but did she have to try to bring it up now? She couldn't get away with it. I wouldn't let her. "I have cavities," I continued. "I admit it. But I'm not going to let them stop me from doing a great job."

I got some funny looks, but it shut up Snotty Ami for

a second. Then Ms. Sigafiss said, "Congratulations, Elyse," and actually smiled at me a little bit, but then she started talking about who knows what so fast that it was like the smile didn't even happen. But it did. I think. *She might not be all bad,* I decided.

I sat down at my desk and traced the letters through my sleeves with my fingers. **A-W-E-S-O-M-E. C-O-O-L. B-E-S-T. S-P-E-C-I-A-L. I-M-P-O-R-T-A-N-T.** Not too shabby. Not too shabby at all.

I bent down to get my notebook out of my backpack (Elyse the Explorer Leader didn't care about whatever Ms. Sigafiss was babbling about, but she was still going to take notes and get good grades) and noticed a crumpled blue paper (the real paper kind, not the Post-it kind) on the floor. My jaw dropped and I felt a surge of dread and excitement both. Was it from the mystery writer? Would it be something cool to do, like being in the fund-raiser show, or something awful, like breaking up Jeg and Kevin? (Maybe this time I'd have to break up Jeg and Liam. Hmm—that might not be so bad.) And what was in it for me, anyway? I had gotten what I wanted. Maybe the note writer just wanted to say hi and congrats or offer some advice for Explorer Leadering. That would be cool. Maybe they would tell me who they were so I could stop wondering! Then I wouldn't even need to do my plan.

Breaking up Jeg and Kevin seemed like such a long time ago. I wished so bad that I had never done it. *But,* I reminded myself, *you didn't do it.* Kevin was going to do it anyway. You just helped speed things up.

Then I noticed a sinking feeling in my stomach, and some awful thoughts popped into my mind. The thing was, what if I had ignored the note writer and skipped that one? What if, without my anonymous motivation, Kevin had decided not to break up with Jeg after all? What if she was still with him today and not with Liam, freeing him up to go out with me again? And also, what the high heels did any of this have to do with me becoming Explorer Leader?

This was what I was (briefly) thinking about as I scooped up the piece of paper and opened it. To my surprise, it was totally, completely blank.

I flipped it over to the other side. Nothing. The one time I had been kinda ready for it, the note was a false alarm. I wasn't sure if I was disappointed or relieved, but when **WORRYWART** crept onto my upper arm, I knew something wasn't completely right with the world.

But Elyse the Explorer Leader ignored the feeling and the word. In fact, she decided officially to put her plan into action that day. She was finally going to figure out who the mystery writer was, and get rid of

WORRYWART and the other annoying words once and for all. Then the incredible Explorer Leader-y words would have all the space they wanted and more.

I took out a thick black marker and scrawled "Who are you?" on the piece of paper. Then I paused. This person, whoever it was, had done something pretty awesome for me, and all I had to say was "Who are you?" I could do better than that.

Thank you for your help and advice. I really appreciate you helping me do what I needed to do to become Explorer Leader and feel a little better. You're awesome! If you'd like to tell me who you are, that would be fantastic.

I wondered how I would deliver this. I hadn't really thought through all the details of the plan. After all, I didn't know who it went to. That was the whole problem. I couldn't really stick it in someone's locker or mailbox or whatever. So what *was* I going to do?

I reviewed how the notes had gotten to me—the first two had been on my locker, one in my reading response journal, one in my teacher's mailbox, one by my table at lunch, one on my seat in English, and one in my backpack. That meant that the writer had to have a schedule similar to mine. This person knew where I would be, when, and made sure to put the notes at times and in places where I would see them.

So really, all I needed to do was continue to follow my own schedule.

Or, I realized, there was another possibility. The note writer might not even go to my school at all, but they could have some kind of connection where they knew someone I knew. Someone who could be a messenger. I knew plenty of people outside of school. My parents. My doctor. My old teachers. I couldn't rule anything—or anyone—out.

Either way, I was going to get to the bottom of this, no matter what it took. This seemed too exciting to take on alone, so right after class I pulled Olivia to the side of the hallway.

"I have to tell you something crazy," I said, and spilled the whole story, every last little blue detail. Well, most of the little blue details. I left out the whole thing about *All this stuff will help you feel better because whoever I am, I know you have CAV.*

"Whoa! That's totally insane!" Olivia said when I was done. "You should have told me sooner. I wonder why that person wanted you to be Explorer Leader so bad? You've got a big fan out there. Or a secret admirer."

I laughed, but it came out kind of quiet and awkward. "I wanted to tell you sooner," I said, ignoring the stuff about why someone would want me to be Explorer Leader. "I didn't know if you'd believe me, and I didn't think you'd want to be friends with a crazy person."

"Elyse, we're all a little crazy," she said, "just in different ways."

Was that a hint? Did she know about CAV? It would have been a good time to tell her, but I couldn't bring myself to do it. Even with all her brothers and sisters and friends in different groups, there was no guarantee that she wouldn't think it was the weirdest thing in the world.

Still, *not* telling her felt weird, too. And wrong.

"Not you," I finally said. "You're not crazy."

She laughed. "Yes, me. Everyone."

I don't know if I believed that, but I let it go and told her the plan to catch the note writer. At the same time, I promised myself in my brain that I'd tell her about CAV, just as soon as I got a better opportunity.

"So," I finished, "I just have to figure out the best time and place to drop my note. And then I have to keep watch and see if anyone picks it up. And I need you to help me."

"Duh." She nodded. "Let's do it tomorrow, at lunch. Everyone will be in the cafeteria. Someone will pick it up. I know it. Also, in case you forgot . . . you're Explorer Leader!"

We jumped up and down a little, and **F-R-I-E-N-D** formed on my wrist. Then came **W-A-N-T-E-D**. They felt so soft and soothing and amazing. I came so close to rolling up my sleeves and showing Olivia, but I chickened out at the last second. I would do it. I would. Just not now. It was better to drop crazy bombs on her one at a time, not all at once.

24
NINJAS

I COULDN'T CONCENTRATE THE WHOLE NEXT MORNING. When lunch finally rolled around, Olivia and I were among the first to get our food and sit down, but I couldn't focus on eating—and it was macaroni day, my favorite, so that was really saying a lot. I scoured the room, trying to figure out who had helped me get this awesome job. No one really gave off that vibe, but it didn't matter, because Olivia and I were going to figure out exactly who it was.

"Okay, I'm making the drop," I told her as we threw away our garbage and edged close to the three stairs you had to climb to leave the cafeteria. "Whoever it is will have to go past here. And when they do . . ."

She looked at me expectantly. "What?"

It was a good question. My plan-planning hadn't

been the best. I'd written my own not-so-mysterious note to the mysterious note writer, but I hadn't thought things through much after that. That was good; I didn't want to think anymore. I had accomplished my goal, really. But I hadn't expected not to know what to do.

I returned Olivia's gaze. "I don't know."

What *would* we do after the person picked up the paper?

"Tell them what I think, I guess. Ask why."

"Are you ready?" Olivia eyed the paper in my hand.

"Let's do it." As we reached the stairs, I slowly opened my fingers just enough to let the paper drop to the floor. I watched it go, sort of in slow motion, like in the movies right before they catch the bad guy.

Olivia grabbed my sleeve and pulled me around the corner. We ducked down low, even though it wasn't really necessary. The person wouldn't be able to see us whether we were two feet tall or ten.

"We should've worn all black today or something," she whispered. "I feel like a ninja."

"I know!" I said. "We should've done backflips and cartwheels into this corner."

"Do you know how to do a backflip?"

"No, do you?"

"No."

We laughed.

"Oh well. Maybe next time," she said.

We carefully leaned around the corner so only our faces were sticking out. We could barely see the piece of paper sitting on the floor, waiting to be picked up. But we could see it enough.

Soon, the flood of footsteps began. We watched foot after foot after foot go over the paper (some stepped right on top of it) and onward up the stairs. None of them stopped. We only saw feet, never hands. No one paused to pick it up.

Until, finally, someone did.

"It's happening!" I grabbed Olivia as we watched a very hairy arm reach down and snatch up the note. It was hairier than any kid's hand would ever be. Unless it was a really, really hairy kid. But I was pretty sure our school didn't have any of those. Mom always said that major changes in hair wouldn't really happen for another year or two, whatever that meant.

"Is that—" I started.

"Mr. Todd!" Olivia whisper-yelled.

Forgetting that we were super-sneaky ninja spies in hiding, we jumped out from behind our corner just in time to see him open the paper and read it.

Though he was frozen in place, his eyes shifted back and forth. *Left, right, left, right.* I watched him scrunch the paper up into a ball, but then he un-scrunched it and read it again. Finally, he tossed it in the recycling bin next to the stairs, looked around, and ran—*yes, ran, in school*—down the hall.

Holy. High. Heels.

25

LEADING

"WILL YOU PASS THE CHIPS, PLEASE?"

Layla smiled and handed them to me across the table. I was discovering more and more perks of being Explorer Leader, but one of the best ones had to be all the snacks at our meetings. So. Many. Snacks.

Mr. Todd—if that was even his real name—grabbed a cookie from a plate being passed around and leaned forward in his chair.

"Let's get down to business, everybody. We've got some serious planning to do. Explorer Leader Elyse, take it away!"

I pulled out my binder (blue, like the color of mysterious notes and suspicious activity) and eyed Mr. Todd to see if he'd have any kind of reaction. It was crazy hard to concentrate on the meeting after what Olivia and I had seen during lunch. I couldn't stop thinking about it. I mean, *Mr. Todd*. Seriously, how much extra time did this dude have on his hands?

Something didn't seem quite right about it, though. He was the king of weirdness, but it was almost *too* weird, even for him. If he didn't think I was good enough for the job, why didn't he give it to someone else? Or tell me, straight out, *Hey, Elyse, you need to be a little cooler of a person first. Why don't you go break up your ex–best friend and her boyfriend? That would totally prove it to me.*

The man was a mystery.

But I was a leader. And it was time to act like one.

"Well, today we're going to focus on the activities," I told the group. "We want to do things that will teach people about the outdoors and wilderness skills and stuff, but we also want activities that get people to talk and work together. What ideas do you guys have?"

"We could discuss important current events, like what everyone's doing over spring break and what music everyone is listening to," Snotty Ami said.

Nice Andy and I exchanged a look. No way could that have been a serious suggestion. But, as a leader, you're not supposed to tell anyone their idea is bad, even if you really want to. At least, that's what it said in one of the "How to Be a Leader" articles Mr. Todd had included in the packet of info he gave me when I got the job.

"Um, interesting idea," I said. "I'm just not sure what it would have to do with the wilderness aspect of our trip."

"We'd do it outside." Snotty Ami flipped her hair over her shoulder.

"I have another idea," said JaShawn. Whew. "How 'bout a trust fall? I've heard those are really cool, and they work best in a big outdoor space where there's sticks and dirt and other bad things you fall on if the person doesn't catch you."

A lot of people nodded and I wrote it down.

"That's a great idea," I said.

Snotty Ami rolled her eyes, but everyone else looked like they agreed.

Feeling good, I took a breath and offered my own idea. "What about a scavenger hunt? People could work in partners or teams and try to find clues hidden outside. We could get compasses and actually use some of that geography stuff we've been learning in social studies."

There were nods of approval all around and even some excited murmurs. My face felt hot, but happy hot. I was leading a meeting, and people liked my idea and wanted to know how I felt about theirs!

As if he could read my mind, Hector leaned over and whispered, "You're a really good leader, Elyse."

L-E-A-D-E-R felt amazing on my leg. The word probably didn't actually make me stronger, but it sure felt like it.

The group added more ideas until I had a whole two pages' worth of activities we could definitely use. Everyone was helping out, but I was taking the notes, running the discussion, *and* keeping an eye on Mr. Number One Suspect, all at the same time.

To be honest, I had no idea I could do so much.

When our meeting was over, everyone (except Snotty Ami, who went straight to a car filled with about a zillion teenagers) walked out together. All the after-school activities were ending, so the parking lot was really crowded. And even though I had just had an awesome meeting, my heart sank lower than the cracked parking-lot pavement when I saw Liam and Jeg walking together, hand in hand, heading toward Liam's brother's car.

Just as quickly as I got **LEADER** and **SMART** and **COOL**, now I was getting **WORTHLESS** and **NOT GOOD ENOUGH** and **UNWANTED**, too. I couldn't help thinking them. Liam never held *my* hand, not once, not ever, not at all during those six days. And I had *really* wanted him to.

But now, with Jeg, she didn't even have to ask him. She didn't even have to scream *Hold my hand!* silently in her mind like I would do, although that had never really been Jeg's style. What was so wrong with my hand?

"Hey, you guys want to come over for some tamales?" Hector asked. "My mom uses my grandma's recipe. Best Mexican food you'll ever have."

Tamales snapped me right back into reality. I've never really been good at pretending that I feel fine when I feel like my guts have been ripped out and stomped on by a high heel, but there were certainly ways to make that feeling hurt a little less. And most of them involved delicious snacks.

But maybe it wasn't just the thought of tamales that made me snap out of the funk. I forced my gaze away from Liam and Jeg and looked at JaShawn, Hector, Layla, and Nice Andy. My friends. Why did I care so much about people who didn't care about me? There were four awesome people staring at me, waiting to hear if I'd go spoil my dinner with them and talk more about our trip.

And as Liam's brother's car drove away with Liam and Jeg inside it, I realized that there was nothing I'd rather do.

26

FUN OR SOMETHING

Elyse the Explorer Leader,

Can you believe it? By the time you read this, you'll be done with the big sixth-grade adventure. All the planning, all the hard work, all the everything—done. I hope you didn't get lost in Minnesota, but I wouldn't be upset if you accidentally left Ms. Sigafiss there. But seriously, I'm dying to know how it all went. Did all the activities go okay? Do people think you did a good job? Do **you** think you did a good job? Here are my other goals:

1. Figure out if the note writer really is Mr. Todd. If it is, I have to do something about these shenanigans. I can't let him run

around pretending everything's totally fine when he owes me a major explanation about the breakup note. Well, about all the notes, but especially that one.

2. Be an awesome Explorer Leader. He chose me, even though it was only because I did all the things he (if he was the note writer) told me to do. And even if it doesn't make all the bad words go away, it still adds a ton of new good ones.
3. Keep doing things, because I'm more fun when I do and people like me better. They clap for me. They cheer. They laugh, and it's actually **with** me, because I'm laughing, too. Because that is what normal people do, and those are my people now. Hooray!

Okay, wish me luck out there. I hope I don't get eaten by a bear.

From,
February Elyse

• • •

People who can successfully close their suitcases after packing for school trips should get a prize. It felt like I had been smushing my stuff down for hours, but my bag was no closer to shutting than it had been when I started.

"I'm not going," I called to Mom. "This is impossible!"

She rushed upstairs in two seconds flat.

"Mom, it's not really an emergency. I'm just telling you."

"Here, let's try again. Or we could bring the bigger suitcase up from downstairs. Or go buy a new one. Or you could take two?"

"I don't know." I looked at my small red bag. It was definitely a challenge, having so much stuff on the packing list but only being allowed a suitcase of a certain size. Plus, there was all the stuff on the packing list you created for yourself. I had packed two sweatshirts instead of the recommended one—but I had to, because I would probably spill something on one, and I needed a spare, just like I needed my fuzziest green knee-high socks, a Costco-size box of chocolate-chip granola bars, a few *Would You Rather . . . ?* books, four rolls of toilet paper (the super-soft kind), and sixteen bottles of nail polish. Regular Elyse probably wouldn't have bothered with all that stuff, but Elyse the Explorer Leader was all about girly bonding and fun supplies for after lights-out.

"Do you really need all this stuff, sweetie?" Mom asked, taking three long-sleeved shirts out of the bag, unfolding them, refolding them in the exact same way I had already folded them, and carefully putting them back.

"Yeah. I really do," I said.

A little later, I finally agreed to remove one roll of toilet paper, four nail polishes, and the fuzzy green knee-high socks. Excuuuuse me for wanting comfort in the frozen wilderness. I didn't think it was so outrageous.

Mom folded the socks and set them gently on my bed. "I promise you'll have them if you need them."

"*Mo-om.* I'll be gone for less than three days. By the time I get them in the mail, it'll be time to leave."

"I'll find a way," she said, a goofy smile spreading across her face. **BABY** sprang onto my lower leg and made itself right at home. Ugh. Maybe I was a baby, but if being a baby meant your mom would send you your fuzzy green knee-high socks if you wanted them, fine. I'd be a baby. Even though it was a pretty itchy thing to be.

An hour later, Mom pulled into the school parking lot and drove in circles forever until she found a spot she liked. Mr. Todd stood in front of the bus with a blue clipboard, looking very official and a little bit like a troublemaker. There had better not be any blue papers on that clipboard. I shot him my very best you-better-not-have-any-blue-papers-on-that-clipboard-and-I-mean-it look.

I'm on to you, dude.

"Hi, Rodney!" Mom smiled widely as we made our way from the car to the bus. I cringed. Your mom should not call your principal by his first name. Your mom shouldn't even know your principal's first name, if you can help it.

I glanced at my phone to read a text from Dad while Mom chatted away with Mr. Todd like they were BFFs.

Good luck. Enjoy. Wear a hat. Love you.

I was going away for three whole days, and that was all he had to say? He hadn't said much more in person before he left for work in the morning. I guess some people just weren't that chatty. Maybe it was time to accept that Dad might be one of them.

"It's been so wonderful seeing everyone!" said Ms. Sigafiss. "We need to get going now, so please give your children a final hug and kiss, then let them get on the bus."

"Well." I turned toward Mom, my heart suddenly beating really fast. I rocked back and forth as **INSECURE** sprouted across my ankle. I felt the prick in my sock, then the familiar itchy jolt of the letters. I am *too* secure! So what if I'm a little nervous about how all this Explorer Leader business will go and how annoying Liam and Jeg will be and what it will be like being away from home for the first time ever? And how I don't know what the rooms will be like or if the beds will be comfy or if the food will be good? So what if I've been excited for this all week—all year, almost—and now I kinda just want to go home and snuggle between Mom and Dad on the couch and watch a movie? That doesn't mean I'm not confident as a person. That just means that at the moment I'm a teeny-tiny bit worried. Yeah. That's all it is.

But if that's all it was, why did I feel like I was going to burst into tears any second?

I expected Mom to pull me in for one of her squish-the-bejeebers-out-of-me hugs, but instead she said, "Be right back!" and jogged away before I could ask what was going on.

"All right, people, you heard Ms. Sigafiss!" Mr. Todd hollered. "Everyone on the bus!" He turned to me.

"How are you doing, Elyse? Ready for some Explorer Leader-ing? This is what it all comes down to. This is your moment! Remember, if you're ever feeling blue, you can always come talk to me. I won't have my couch with me this trip, though. It didn't quite fit in my suitcase."

"Mm-kay." I didn't smile.

Mom rushed to the bus, an oversize duffel bag in her

hands. *Wait, why does Mom have a duffel?* I told her I wasn't allowed to have a second bag.

Then it hit me. The bag was not for me.

"Surprise!" Mom threw her free arm around my shoulders. "I'm coming with you!"

"You're . . . what?"

"Rodney—er, Mr. Todd—called me yesterday. Apparently there weren't enough chaperones signed up, and he thought I might be interested."

I glared at Mr. Todd. What *was* this? It didn't make any sense that he'd do all that work with the notes to make me Explorer Leader and then go and invite my mom along on the trip. If he *had* written the notes, he must have changed his mind about me. Maybe he didn't really think I could do it on my own after all.

He was still standing in front of the bus, smiling away, checking names off the list on his clipboard like it was the most fun he'd ever had in his life. When he caught my eye, he smiled and waved like we were old pals.

"I thought it'd be a fun surprise . . . I thought you'd want me to come." Mom sighed. "It's a scary new experience for you. I called Dr. Patel about it, and he agreed that it would be smart. Wouldn't it be nice to have me around, you know, just in case? I won't embarrass you."

Usually when she said she wouldn't embarrass me, it

was a sure sign that she was going to embarrass me. Like really bad. But I looked at her face; she was so hopeful, and the last thing I wanted to do was hurt her feelings.

And there was the annoying fact that a teeny tiny, microscopic part of me might maybe want her around maybe for a little teeny tiny bit of time. Like an hour. Or two. Two and a half, tops. Just till the annoying lump in my throat went away.

"Fine." I shrugged. "If that's what you want to do."

Her face lit up. "It's going to be so fun, sweetie!"

Yeah, fun. Or something.

27

ROOMIES

"IT APPEARS THAT MY MOM IS A LAST-MINUTE CHAPERONE," I told Olivia after I slid into a seat next to her.

"Oh," she said sympathetically. "Sorry." I noticed she didn't pat my leg. That was nice. Then she changed the subject and started talking about a funny show she'd seen on TV last night. That was pretty nice, too.

It was hard not having Jeg as a best friend anymore, but I was beginning to think that maybe Olivia would be a good replacement, even if it wasn't quite the same.

We played MASH the rest of the way to Minnesota. (MASH stands for *mansion, apartment, shack, house.* When you play the game, you find out which one you're going to live in when you grow up, and you find out a lot of other important things, too.) By the end of the drive, we had discovered that when we grew up, Olivia was going to live in a mansion in Hawaii with her husband (Nice Andy—ha, ha!) and her seventeen kids and her pet llama named Ferdinand Wellington the Third. I was going to live in an apartment at the North Pole with my husband (Kevin—ew), our thirty-three kids, and two pet unicorns named Fifi and Gigi. The future was looking weird.

After several hours, the bus slowed down as it turned onto a dusty, gravelly path. Big brown snow-covered trees lined both sides of the road. The bus went slower and slower. Each time I thought it was going to pull over, it kept on going, like the little engine that could.

After what seemed like a billion years, the bus finally came to a stop in an empty parking lot.

"Everyone stay seated!" Mr. Todd instructed as he got off the bus, but no one did. We were way too antsy. The drive had been *six* hours, after all.

I shook out my foot a little bit. It still felt itchy from **INSECURE**. After Mr. Todd had invited Mom, **UNABLE** was there, too. He didn't truly believe I could do it on my own. Neither did Mom.

So maybe they were right, and I couldn't.

I guess I'd find out soon enough.

Kevin stood and ran up and down the bus's aisle. Mike stuck out his hand for a high five as Kevin passed, and soon everyone else did, too. I stretched my arms in both directions, careful not to accidentally smack anyone in the face. I was a very polite stretcher. You could not say the same for most people. Like Liam. Liam, I noticed, was kind of an inconsiderate stretcher. He was doing, like, some kind of yoga thing (show-off) with one leg going sideways and one arm poised behind his head with the elbow sticking out, practically jabbing Olivia in the ear.

"Okay," said Mr. Todd, as he climbed back on the bus. "I appreciate your patience. Let's everyone get ready to head to our cabins. There will be two people to a room and eight to a cabin, plus a chaperone. Jeg and Elyse, cabin one, room one. Hannah and Hannah, cabin one, room two . . ."

His mouth kept moving, but I couldn't hear anything after he said my name. I squeezed my eyes shut, hoping no one would see the tears that had welled up way too fast. I thought being Explorer Leader guaranteed me my own room. Sure, no one had ever told me *officially*, but it just seemed like a natural perk of the job. Kings and queens of school dances got crowns. Captains of sports teams got special sweatshirts. And Explorer Leaders of wilderness adventures should get their own rooms. It was simple as that.

And of all the roommates in the entire world I could get—Jeg? It would be so awkward. We had hardly said a word to each other since her party. Being trapped in a room together for three days would be torture. And that meant I'd have to change in front of her, too. She hadn't seen my words since last year, when she was nice. Now she was the kind of person who might make fun of them, threaten to tell other people, and try to make them worse. On purpose.

I felt Mom's eyes on me from the way front of the bus. She didn't know everything, but she had definitely noticed Jeg and I weren't hanging out much—or at all—anymore. Mom pushed her way back to my seat and slid in next to me, forcing Olivia to scoot all the way over to the window.

"*Mom!* What are you doing?" Practically everyone was looking at us as they lined up to get off the bus. Mom stood out like a fuzzy orange sock in a basket of green ones.

"I'm just checking on you, sweetie," she whispered. "I know the roommate announcement caught you off guard. Do you want me to talk to Mr. Todd about it and see if we can figure something out?"

I sniffled. I *did*, but wouldn't that prove exactly what both of them thought, that I couldn't do anything for myself? Even though I was the Explorer Leader?

Yes, I said in my brain. "No," I whispered back, and sniffled again.

Mom looked at me for a long time, but finally got up and went back to her real spot on the bus.

Olivia turned to me as soon as Mom went away. "Are you okay? I know you and Jeg aren't BFFs anymore, but it's only for a few days. And we'll be outside most of the time anyway!"

It was easy for her to say. As nice as Olivia was, she still didn't know the truth about me. She didn't get why this was such a huge problem. And I was still too scared to tell her.

I tried to smile. "Yeah, you're right. I know."

When everyone was off the bus, Snotty Ami dragged Jeg up to Mr. Todd. I didn't realize that other people would be as upset about the roommate assignment as I was. Snotty Ami didn't know she was doing me a favor, but that's exactly what was happening. I felt a very small twinge of appreciation for her.

"There has been a mistake," she insisted, with Jeg nodding in agreement and me watching from not too far away. I had never seen Snotty Ami look so upset. Her face was bright red and I could practically see steam coming out of her snotty ears. "I'm not supposed to be with some random person I barely know. Jeggie was supposed to be my roomie, not that loser's." She muttered those last three words under her breath and glanced in my direction. I looked down, not wanting anyone to see me scowl as **LOSER** formed sharply on my thigh. Ouch. There wasn't enough anti-itch cream in the universe for that one. *Of course* Snotty Ami couldn't just do me a favor she didn't know she was doing and be nice about it. She had to be the only person in the world who didn't care that I was the Explorer Leader and *it was basically the rule that you were supposed to be nice to the Explorer Leader.*

"Are you okay?" Mom popped out of nowhere and stroked my arm. "I saw you wince. What did she call you? I am going to have a word with that girl's mother when we get back. Here, I brought the extra-strength kind." She pulled a gigantic tube of something gross and embarrassing from her purse.

"Mom!" I jerked away, super aware of everyone looking at the Explorer Leader about to be gooped up by her mommy. Sitting by her on the bus for a few minutes was one thing, but this was not okay. "I'm fine. I'm used to it. I don't want the lotion."

"There weren't any mistakes," Mr. Todd told Snotty Ami. "Your roommate is your roommate. No changes. It is what it is. Don't be blue. And don't be so mean, either. I think you and I need to have a chat when we get back to school."

Snotty Ami snottily sulked away. For once, I wished she had gotten what she wanted.

"Should we go?" Jeg crept up to me and pointed to the big brown cabin on our right.

"I guess." I couldn't bring myself to look at her. Plus, **LOSER** was driving me crazy, and all I could think about was getting into our room so I could sneakily unpeel some layers and scratch the bejeebers out of it.

Ms. Sigafiss finished unloading the bags, so we grabbed ours and walked together in silence. Jeg held the door open for me, and I went through without saying thank you for maybe the first time in my entire life. I was just not in a thank-you kind of mood.

The cabin was huge. It had a wide entryway, a giant living room when you first walked in, and rooms going every which way. We found the door with a big "Room 1" sign on it and went inside. It was a teeny space, like the size of my bedroom. There were skinny bunk beds along one wall and two dressers along the other. The whole room—the whole cabin, really—practically screamed, *If you forget to close the door, you'll get eaten by a bear. Have fun!* Looking around the room, I decided that it might not have been so fun on my own after all. In fact, it might have been the creepiest thing ever. But I was still more worried than relieved.

"I like it in here," Jeg said. "It's cozy."

"Yup." I couldn't think of what else to say, so I pretended to be really interested in my suitcase. I unzipped it, thinking maybe I could show Jeg some of the nail polish I brought.

But that's not what was right on top, like it was supposed to be.

I stared for a second in complete disbelief. *Another one?* I was so surprised that I didn't even notice Jeg come up behind me.

"You okay?" She peeked over my shoulder. "OMG, that's not, like, another one of those creepy notes, is it? Like the one you got at the beginning of the year?" She nudged me. "You never told me what that note said."

And I never will.

Although she wasn't acting totally snotty at the moment.

And it might be okay to tell someone else. She might think of something that Olivia and I hadn't. And I was kind of about to burst; it was just too weird that this was still going on.

I quickly read the note to myself, then turned around to face her. This was either a brilliant idea or a huge mistake.

"I've been getting them all year. They say nice things. Sometimes they tell me things I have to do."

I held this one up so she could see it.

Have a great trip, Elyse! You've worked hard and deserve to enjoy every minute.

Remember, someone is always going to have something bad to say. But can you remember the good you've done? The good you ARE?

"Olivia and I think it's Mr. Todd," I said once she finished reading.

For once, Jeg was totally speechless. "Oh . . . em—" she started, but was interrupted when the door to our room flung open.

It was Ms. Sigafiss, looking like a bear in her super-long, dark winter coat. If only there were a way to make sure *she* stayed out of our cabin.

"First activity is outside in two minutes," she growled.

Jeg and I looked at each other and smiled.

"Gee!" she whispered as we followed Ms. Sigafiss out the door.

Oh-em-gee was right.

Jeg and I had a secret for the first time in months.

And it felt really, really good.

28

FACECICLES

OUTSIDE, EVERYONE GATHERED AROUND A TALL SILVER flagpole. Except for dozens of small cabins scattered around, there were no buildings to be found—only open spaces, covered in fluffy white snow. If I had been less cranky, I probably would have liked it. It might have reminded me of a perfect winter wonderland like the ones you see in snow globes and in amazing movies like *Frosty the Snowman*.

"All right, people." Mr. Todd faced the group. "Welcome to the sixth-grade adventure! We have a lot of fun challenges planned for you this weekend. I'll let our Explorer Leader come tell you about your first activity."

Everyone cheered like crazy except for Snotty Ami. Her snotty face snarled like someone told her she could never go shopping ever again. A small smile tugged at my lips and my ankle started feeling like an ankle again instead of one giant mosquito bite. I rushed up to stand by Mr. Todd, energized by everyone's excitement. Even if no one really believed I could do this, here I was, doing this.

"Hi," I said. "Um—"

"Speak up, sweetie!" Mom called in such a loud voice that probably all the animals in the woods could hear.

I shot her a look. *Really, Mom?*

Now everyone was looking at me, waiting.

"Come on, Elyse!" Jeg started clapping again, so everyone else did, too.

Okay. I could do this.

"We're going on a scavenger hunt," I said in a louder voice. "The camp ranger hid a bunch of clues all over the place. Working with a partner whose name you'll draw out of a hat, you have to follow your clues, and whoever gets back first wins. Oh, and"—I smiled—"you can only bring a walkie-talkie to communicate with the adults, a small snack, a compass, and a water bottle. That's it. No phones."

Everyone groaned. I knew they'd hate that part.

"How are we supposed to know where we're going without a phone?" Snotty Ami whined. She had clearly not been paying attention in our meetings.

"Meet the compass," Ms. Sigafiss said, dropping one in Ami's hand. "The original Google Maps."

Snotty Ami pouted and I stifled a giggle. Who knew Ms. Sigafiss had a sense of humor?

Mr. Todd held out a blue baseball hat filled with slips of paper.

"Everyone's names are in here," he said. "Good luck! Liam, why don't you come pick first?"

A bunch of guys cheered for Liam as he groaned softly. Jeg whispered something to him and they both glanced at me. She wasn't telling him about the blue notes, was she? I should've known there was no way Jeg could (or would) keep a secret for me anymore. He tried to pull away and go up to the hat, but she clutched his hand like he was going to be fed to an alligator when she let go. I would never hold Nice Andy's hand like that, even if he really *was* about to be alligator food.

Liam finally escaped and his arm dove into the hat. It was the same arm that had done all that fancy yoga on the bus, the same one that had once rested around my shoulder. The same arm attached to the hand I had never gotten to hold.

It's funny how someone can put his arm around you but never hold your hand. Holding hands seems like the most basic thing, but maybe it's actually arm-around-ing. Maybe I don't know anything about romance at all.

He pulled out a small slip of blue paper and stared at it for a second before saying anything out loud.

"Elyse," he said in a depressed way that made me think maybe he really was going to be fed to an alligator, but that was confusing because I was pretty sure I hadn't arranged for any alligators to join us on this trip. Wait a second. Elyse? Uh-oh.

"Go!" Olivia pushed me forward and gave me an encouraging look.

"Good luck!" Mr. Todd handed me a small slip of blue paper that must have been our first clue.

"Shall we get this over with?" Liam approached me, little pieces of his hair flopping around in the wind. "The wilderness is waiting."

"We shall," I answered, opening the clue. Maybe I could just pretend he wasn't here. Then I wouldn't have to worry about liking him and hating him at the same time and the confusion that came along with that. Maybe I could still have fun. Somehow.

Follow the snow eight hundred paces
In the direction due west.
Turn right, look up.
Will you pass this test?

"I thought tests were just for school," I said with a wobbly voice. I was starting to regret letting the teachers write the clues for the scavenger hunt. My armpits were soaking wet, even though there were like twenty-nine layers of clothes separating me from them. This was not the time to be nervous. And Liam was not the right person to be nervous around. He didn't even spare me a fake laugh.

"Let's go," he said, giving me a look like *I* was the crazy person here.

We started walking away from the group, which was no easy task. The snow was up to our knees, and it made walking really difficult.

"Are we going the right way?" I asked.

Liam stared at the compass like he was waiting for it to do a trick. "Yup."

"Okay."

I trudged on behind him. With his long legs, it was hard to tell if he was purposely walking ahead of me or if it just happened that way by accident. I jogged a little to catch up, but it wasn't easy. Even my jogging steps couldn't keep up with his regular steps.

"Slow down!" I panted.

He didn't.

"Liam! Hello! People are talking to you!"

"I want to get to the clue," he muttered.

"And what do you think I want, exactly? To bake some pie?"

He snorted and picked up his pace. Snow came down,

fast and furious. I caught a few flakes with my tongue, thinking it would be smart to keep hydrated, considering I was going to have to run a marathon to keep up with my partner.

"Seriously, can you slow down? Please? I'm supposed to be the one mad at you, here. But I stink at being mad, so you're safe."

"I don't care if you're mad," he said as he tied his thick maroon scarf a little tighter.

"Then what? What is your deal? Why are you being this way?"

"This is me," he said. "Sorry if I bug you. Jeg doesn't seem to mind me too much. Thanks for that."

I had no idea what that meant. Maybe I had heard him wrong. He was pretty far ahead of me, after all. I chased him the best I could. Moving was getting harder and harder as the snow was coming down faster and faster. Worse, there didn't seem to be any clues in sight.

Actually, there didn't seem to be *anything* in sight.

"Are you sure you know where we're going?" I asked.

Then I silently replayed what he had said. It had definitely sounded like a thanks, but that didn't make any sense. I thought back to Jeg's party. He had thanked me then, too. Either he was way into politeness all of a sudden or something really weird was going on.

"Wait. Why did you thank me?"

"Because you made it happen." He finally stopped moving, turned, and looked me right in the eyes. His normally pale face was a little pink, and his eyes were the same greenish brown as usual. If anything, they were brighter compared to the dull gray of the sky.

The sky got darker and darker as the snow continued to come down. The pretty flakes from before had turned to hard, angry chunks. I shivered in my twenty-nine layers. The weather was changing, and not for the better.

"What do you mean, I made it happen? What did I make happen?"

"You did what I said, didn't you?" he asked. "From the note?"

"What note?" The realization hit me like a snowball. I stopped dead in my tracks.

It wasn't possible.

The notes were from Mr. Todd, most likely. They were written on his favorite blue paper. He picked up the note I left as bait. He took off running down the hall. It *had* to be him. There was proof!

Unless—unless Liam had blue paper, too. Mr. Todd didn't really *own* the color blue, after all.

And Mr. Todd could have only picked up the bait because he's the kind of guy who picks up paper from the ground, like Olivia said. It *was* super weird that he would ask me to break up Jeg and Kevin. That whole thing kept giving my gut the funny feeling that something was off.

My whole body felt hollow, like someone had taken a vacuum and sucked all the life right out of me. It was like Liam was breaking up with me all over again.

"The note I wrote you." He laughed, then turned and kept walking. "The one where I told you to break up Jeg and Kevin. And look at you now, Miss Explorer Leader. And look at me, going out with the hottest, coolest girl in school. I'm finally popular. We both got what we wanted. We both won."

I couldn't believe what I was hearing. How could he do this?

"You dropped that note in the cafeteria?" I asked. "Why there? Why then?"

"I dunno." He shrugged. "Had it in my pocket forever. You were close by and it seemed like a good chance to drop it."

"But what about the others?" I asked.

"The other what?"

My stomach got all knotty as I remembered something I hadn't given much thought: the way the note about breaking up Jeg and Kevin looked. That was the only note that was on a Post-it instead of a piece of regular paper. That was the only note that was handwritten, not typed.

That note was different.

"The other notes. There were a lot of them."

"Oh, right. Those. Yeah, those weren't me. I just saw one stuck to your locker, and I read it, and I got ideas." He smiled like he was really proud of himself.

Neither of us said anything. Liam looked down at his boots.

"Do you know who wrote the other ones? Was it Mr. Todd?"

"I dunno," he said. "I didn't see the person, just the paper. I don't think Mr. Todd would do it, though. Doesn't seem like his kind of thing."

We stood there in silence for another minute, both of us looking at the ground.

"So . . . do you want to, like, apologize?" I asked.

But he wasn't listening. He was looking down at the compass, and his shoulders were heaving up and down like he was really worried about something.

"I think we went the wrong way," he said with a gulp.

"We have a walkie-talkie," I practically whispered. "We can call a teacher and get help."

The sky was now a deep, dark black. The other teams were probably on their way back with all the clues in tow, getting ready for an awesome dinner of grilled cheese and tomato soup with triple-chocolate cupcakes for dessert (my idea, thank you very much—even Snotty Ami had agreed with that one).

The other teams probably actually used their brains and didn't just blindly follow people who were tall and cute and had eyes like little kiwis and looked like official explorers in their fancy thick scarves and hiker-guy boots and giant jackets. People who had said they knew where they were going.

Anger bubbled up inside of me. *How could he?*

But worse than feeling furious with Liam, I was mad at myself for trusting him and liking him. For going along with his note and doing what it said, even when it felt wrong.

I looked ahead and realized that Liam was nowhere to be found. The dark sky had swallowed him whole, fancy hiker-guy boots and all.

"Liam?" I called, and got no answer.

A shiver went down my spine, and not just because it was freezing. My heart pounded and my whole body got sweaty despite the cold.

"Liam?" I yelled again, louder this time. Then again. "LIAM!"

Nothing.

It was getting darker and darker. The snow was coming down furiously, and even if I had a hundred tongues I'd never be able to catch it all and get it out of the way so I could see clearly. No matter what direction I turned, it was like staring into an angry marshmallow.

I shivered again, and thoughts of fuzzy socks flashed through my mind. Would I ever see my green knee-highs again? Would I ever see anything again besides snow?

I couldn't help it; I started to cry, but even that was a failure, because the second the tears dropped out of my eyes and onto my cheeks, they froze into mini icicles on my face. *Facecicles.* I was too scared and sad to laugh at my hilarious new word.

"Okay. It's going to be okay." My voice shook with each word I spoke to myself. "It's cold and dark and scary and you are not carrying any of the explorer supplies, but you will be okay. You just have to go back the way you came."

Except—all the ways looked the same. Even if I could tell which direction I had come from, I wouldn't have known, because the only thing I'd looked at the whole time was the back of Liam's thick brown jacket. And a jacket isn't exactly a landmark.

I traced over **UNWANTED** with a frozen finger. Even through twenty-nine layers, each letter still managed to feel like a little rash of doom. I let out a loud whimper. My legs throbbed, and the rest of me felt heavy and empty at the same time. What I wouldn't give for some of Mom's nasty anti-itch goop right now. I was hungry, thirsty, tired, and totally, completely alone.

For once, I hated the quiet. It reminded me that no one was coming to save me.

"Help!" I shouted at the top of my lungs. *Good luck with that,* I imagined the snow replying.

Liam had never cared about me. He just wanted to go out with Jeg.

Only people like Nice Andy cared about me.

People like Liam would never, ever like me. Ever.

And why should they? Yeah, I was Explorer Leader, but Mom and Mr. Todd didn't really think I could do it alone.

And they were right.

I burst into a whole new set of tears, not caring about the facecicles that were sure to form.

I plopped down in the snow right where I was. My butt froze immediately; snow seeped right through my snow pants and probably my regular pants, too, and maybe even my underwear.

That was a stupid thing to do, sitting down.

I cried more. Everything I did was so stupid.

The word formed and I knew it was coming and I didn't even care. When it jabbed me, I jabbed it right back with my fingers, making everything itch more.

For a few minutes, I just sat there like a lump. Poking

myself. Crying. Feeling like the biggest failure in the history of failures.

After a little while, the wind slowed down slightly, and the snow came down lighter and flakier. I made myself get up, and then I dusted off as much snow from my cold, wet body as I could.

I had to move, I figured. I had to try. Staying in that spot forever wasn't going to do anything.

I glanced up at the dark, hazy sky. In social studies we'd talked about the North Star and how you can use it to help you if you're lost.

We hadn't talked about what to do if you couldn't see it, though. Seriously not cool, snowstorm.

A big gust of wind blew in my face, sending my hair flying around my head. There had been wind before, but it was the nice kind of wind that felt like it was patting me on the back and pushing me forward.

Wait. That was it!

If Liam and I had set off going west, and there wasn't wind in my face, but now there was, I must have turned around. That meant that I was facing the right way. To get back, I just had to walk into the wind. Which would be kind of awful, but not nearly as awful as getting ditched.

As I took one step and then another, I thought back to what Liam had said about how he had only written one of the notes after someone else—*not Mr. Todd*, in his opinion—had given him the idea.

It was the same thing I'd started thinking. It just didn't add up for the notes to be from the principal. And if that were true, and the rest of the notes weren't from Mr. Todd, that meant there was someone out there who actually really did want me to be Explorer Leader. Who believed, against all odds, that I could do it. That I could do anything.

And I was letting that person down.

I was letting *me* down.

And really, up until this point, I had done a pretty good job as Explorer Leader. I had taken charge at the meetings. I'd kept track of a whole bunch of details in my fancy Explorer Leader binder. I'd planned fun things. A couple of weeks ago, Mr. Todd had finally put my picture in that blank poster with the question mark, and right away people had started filling it in with compliments about what a good leader I was.

Maybe they weren't just doing that because I had the job and they wanted me to listen to their ideas. Maybe they really meant the compliments. I'd earned them, hadn't I?

"You planned a great trip," I said out loud. Totally dorky, but no one was really listening except for the snow-covered trees, and they probably wouldn't tell anyone.

"You're brave to stay in a room with Jeg and not let Mom talk Mr. Todd into changing it. You're nice to people even when they're not nice to you. And you look kind of adorable in all of your winter gear, even though it makes you feel very poofy."

I lunged forward as I talked, feeling a little better and lighter as **BRAVE**, **NICE**, and **ADORABLE** formed and the itchiness subsided. I plodded on, taking one step after another, and as I did I began to hear faint voices off in the distance. I couldn't make out what they were saying, but they were definitely there. I took a huge, relieved breath. I was going the right way. Holy. High. Heels.

I continued going toward the voices, and as I did, Mr. Todd's words from a long time ago echoed in my mind.

I have a lot more hair than most people.

I have a lot more hair than most people.

I have a lot more hair than most people.

He had more hair than most people.

And I had words on my body.

And sometimes, they were bad ones.

And then it occurred to me: So what?

I moved closer to the voices, and most all of my itchiness went away as I realized I was getting back to camp, somehow, all by myself. Me. Elyse. With no help, no compass, no phone, no blue notes, no boy, no friends. Just me.

In place of the itchiness, I felt something else, something amazing. I didn't know what it was, but I wanted it to last forever.

A blast of energy spiraled through my whole body and I didn't even notice that all my clothes were sopping wet. I smiled through chattering teeth and started running—running!—through the mountains of snow toward the voices.

Soon, I could make out actual words, and I sprinted toward them with all the strength I could muster. I could do this. I had made it this far, and now I was almost there.

With one final push, I flew through a thin crest of trees and found myself right in front of the flagpole, a sight that had seemed so regular hours ago. Now it was the best, most amazing flagpole I had ever seen in my entire life. I hugged it as tightly as I could.

"Elyse!" Mom's eyes were red and puffy, and she had facecicles, too. Giant ones. She took me in her arms, and I let myself fall into them and sigh into their warmth without caring who saw or what they thought.

I had found my way.

29

OKAY

WHEN I CAME OUT OF THE HUG, I SAW ADULTS ALL OVER the place, shouting into their walkie-talkies and texting like their thumbs were on fire. "She's okay!" I heard. "She's back!" It was nice to know they'd all been so concerned about me, but the only person I could concentrate on was Liam. He stood there with his jaw practically on the ground. Was he surprised to see me? What'd he expect, that I'd stay there forever waiting for him to come back and rescue me? That I'd turn into a human ice cube and spend the rest of my days in the Minnesota wilderness?

Jeg, Olivia, Hannah, and Hannah came running up to me. Their hands were full with grilled cheese and cupcakes.

"We were so worried!" Hannah Z. said. She handed over a warm chocolate bundle of joy.

"Ladies, this is a lovely thought, but I think Elyse needs blankets first. And warm clothes," Mr. Todd suggested.

"No, cupcakes will work," I said through my frozen mouth, and everyone laughed.

"I see the ordeal hasn't harmed her sense of humor!" Mr. Todd chuckled. "But really, Elyse, are you all right? We were so concerned. Your mom was this close to having the police come out here. What happened?"

"I'm okay," I said. I snuggled back into Mom's arms. "But I am a little blue." I pointed to my wet blue jacket. "A lot blue, actually. And I don't really know what happened . . . I guess I just kinda veered off-course a little. My partner wasn't so good at sharing the compass. Or sticking around."

Mr. Todd shot Liam a look like he was in huge trouble, and Liam stared down at the ground. "We'll talk about that later. And I mean seriously talk, Liam. For now, I'll grab blankets while you go change, Elyse. Then we'll meet in the dinner cabin."

Mom led me to my cabin without saying a word. She started a fire and carefully helped me peel off wet layer after wet layer until you could finally see my cold, red skin.

She went over to her bag and pulled something out. I was bracing myself for a goop-down (I didn't have that many bad words left, but Mom would probably slather me anyway) when she opened her hands and showed me what she was holding: my fuzzy green knee-high socks!

"I thought we should have these here," Mom said. "Just in case."

"Thanks." I grinned from ear to ear as I felt the new word that spread across my entire arm, all the way from my hand to my shoulder: **OKAY**.

I threw on a sweatshirt, some sweatpants, and the fuzzy socks. When I got back, everyone had already finished dinner, but a huge crowd swarmed me in the dinner cabin as I polished off three grilled cheese sandwiches, two enormous bowls of tomato soup (mmm, soup), and two and a half gooey chocolate cupcakes. Hey, I earned it.

"Were you scared?" Paige asked.

"Did you see any bears?" asked Kevin.

"I wish you had told me you were going to be late," Ms. Sigafiss insisted. "I would have appreciated knowing I'd have to prepare so many grilled cheese sandwiches so long after dinnertime."

"It wasn't exactly something I planned," I said, and everyone laughed, even her. I wondered if the grilled cheese comment was actually her way of trying to be funny.

"Give Elyse some space," said Mr. Todd. "She's had a very long night. It's getting pretty late. Let's all start heading to our cabins."

People slowly trickled out in small groups until no one remained except Mom and Jeg.

"Sweetie, you should really get to sleep," Mom said. Her arm was still around my shoulder. It was starting to feel a little heavy. "Let me know if you need anything tonight, okay? You can wake me anytime. I'm just a few cabins over from you."

"Okay," I said. I jumped to my feet and shook her arm off in the process.

To my surprise, Jeg grabbed my arm and linked hers through my elbow, like we used to do when we were little. Like she'd done all year with Snotty Ami.

"I'll take good care of her, Mrs. Everett," she promised.

We stepped outside. It was still cold, dark, and windy, but I wasn't scared. It was hard to believe that I had just been all alone out there, not sure if I would live to eat grilled cheese. It all seemed like such a long time ago.

For a few minutes, the only sound was our boots crunching in the snow.

"You know," I finally said as I stepped on a small piece of ice, crushing it beneath my foot. "Liam isn't so nice. He totally ditched me out there."

"I know," Jeg mumbled.

"And it kinda seemed like you were telling him about the notes before we left on the scavenger hunt. Were you?"

"No!" She pushed her scarf out of her face. "Of course not. I was just telling him I was glad I got you for a roommate. And that I was gonna miss him." Her face reddened. "I'm really sorry, Elyse. For being with him. I just wanted to go out with someone. Ami and everyone told me I should because they all had boyfriends, so I needed one, too, and he was interested. I thought I would be with Kevin forever, but I guess not."

We pushed open the door to our cabin and started flinging off our winter clothes, sending them flying in every direction. The heat from the fire Mom had made in our cabin earlier felt amazing.

I watched Jeg's stuff scatter. All of her winter clothes were different than they used to be. When we were little kids—and even up until last year—she had the craziest snow stuff I'd ever seen. She'd wear zebra-striped snow pants, rainbow coats, mittens with sequins, the works.

But now all of her stuff was so plain, so regular. So not Jeg.

A funny feeling crept up in my gut again, and I knew it wanted me to come clean about the part I had played in her breakup with Kevin. Even though I hadn't *really* been responsible for them breaking up. Even though she didn't really deserve my apology. I was going to do it anyway.

"Jeg," I said, "it's kind of a long story, but I sort of

mentioned to Kevin that it might be a good idea to break up with you. It was one of the mystery notes that suggested it, actually, but it was my choice to do it, and I want you to know that I'm really sorry."

I didn't mention that the writer of this particular mysterious note wasn't so mysterious anymore. I'd already messed up one of her relationships; I wasn't going to say any more about this one. All I could do was hope she'd figure Liam out before he could make her sad.

I slipped off my sweatshirt and threw it on the bottom bunk. Before I knew it, I was down to my very bottom layer, a thin dark gray T-shirt, and she could see the giant **OKAY** trailing down my arm. For some reason, I wasn't worried about it anymore.

"Whoa," Jeg said, looking at me. I looked back at her, and maybe it was the weird shadows in the cabin, but I could've sworn that our Best Friends necklace was tucked under her shirt.

She turned away from me, slipped on her pajamas, and climbed into the top bunk. "I haven't seen those words in a while. You look really cool!" Then she sighed. "It's okay, El. I told Kevin I kissed Pierre, and that's why he broke up with me. It had nothing to do with you. It's super weird that one of Mr. Todd's notes would ask you to do that, though. What does the principal care who's going out with who?"

"Dunno," I said. "Maybe he really wants to be a matchmaker instead of a principal."

Jeg giggled. "He could get his own TV show! *Middle School Matchmaker.*"

I laughed and took a happy deep breath. I still wasn't Jeg's biggest fan in the world, but there was something nice about knowing that she wasn't mad at me. She may have said more stuff after that, but I'm not quite sure because I fell asleep the second my head touched the pillow.

• • •

Everyone was extra nice to me after I'd survived getting lost on the scavenger hunt. The next day, Jeg invited me to sit with her and the Loud Crowd at breakfast, and I did, and when Snotty Ami looked over at Hannah B. at the next table and asked us, "Do you think she wears a bra because she needs one or because she wants one?" Jeg very politely turned to me and said, "Elyse, what do you think?" I didn't really know what the right answer was, and I didn't want to say anything mean about Hannah. So I just kind of smiled and shrugged, and that must have been the right answer because Snotty Ami was all "Yeah" and they smiled at me like I was doing a good job.

Then I hung out with Hannah, Hannah, and Olivia, and I could just relax and talk about normal things like cupcakes and books and not have to worry if I was getting answers right or not.

After that, I sat by the fireplace for a while, all by myself, and I didn't even sneak off like I usually do at lunch. I just told people I wanted to be alone for a little bit, and they said okay. I still don't know if they thought it was weird or not. Maybe they did. But that's their opinion, not mine.

It felt good to think like that.

Then, during the trust fall, people were actually fighting over who got to be my partner. I picked Nice Andy.

"You're so awesome and cool!" he told me before he fell into my arms.

"Thanks!" I said. Then I said "Oof!" and caught him, though I stumbled backward a little bit (okay, a lot) in the process. **AWESOME** and **COOL** were still on my arms, right where he had put them, but they seemed to be staying put whether he repeated them or not.

After the trust fall, Mr. Todd made a huge deal about presenting me with my official Explorer Leader poster in front of everybody. It was weird—the poster had seemed so important before, but I had almost forgotten about it until he unrolled it and waved it up in the air like a big flag.

And there it was. My face. Surrounded by all the good words I'd wanted so bad. **FUNNY. SMART. HELPFUL. FRIENDLY. CREATIVE. ORGANIZED. GREAT LEADER.** They went on forever.

The poster looked exactly like I'd hoped it would, but there was something confusing about it. All these words, these amazing qualities that I thought being Explorer Leader would help me to be—well, wasn't I a lot of them before?

Actually, not to toot my own horn or anything, but wasn't I *all* of them before?

I smiled and took the poster from Mr. Todd as everyone clapped. Suddenly everything was so obvious: the mystery notes, being Explorer Leader—they were great, but they didn't magically turn me into the girl on the poster with the good words swirling around her head. She was the person I already was. Everything else just helped me notice.

And with the poster tucked in my arms and the words echoing in my mind, I knew I'd never forget.

"I wish I had one of those," Snotty Ami said in a quiet voice as the clapping died down. I glanced at her over my shoulder and saw that she hadn't said that to a friend—she'd said it to the ground. Her eyes refused to meet anyone else's. She didn't look nearly as cool as she usually did when she was surrounded by everybody. Now she just looked normal. Maybe even sort of sad.

She looked like a girl who just really needed some compliments.

I whispered something to Mr. Todd, and he nodded. Then he disappeared into a cabin for a minute and came back with a bunch of markers and a thick stack of blue papers.

"Spontaneous new activity, courtesy of our Explorer Leader," he said, and I quickly sat everybody down at the picnic tables and explained it. I couldn't believe an idea like this had just popped into my mind, and that I'd been brave enough to tell it to Mr. Todd and now we were really doing it.

Actually, maybe I *could* believe it.

Ten minutes later, we were done. The other posters weren't as big and fancy as my poster, but what they said was more important than what they looked like. Everybody put their names at the top of their papers and left them on the tables, and then everyone walked around and wrote compliments on them. Now everybody had their own mini posters, filled with a bunch of good words from a bunch of different people.

It was so fun looking at all the papers that I accidentally left my poster behind when it was time to go have a snack inside.

Snotty Ami—or maybe just regular Ami, actually—ran up to me, holding it.

"You forgot this," she said in a totally regular, non-snotty kind of way.

"Thanks," I said.

"Yeah, thanks to you, too," she said.

And she smiled.

30

OLIVIA AND THE WORDS

I GLANCED OVER AT THE ADULTS. THEY ALL HUDDLED together and talked in low, serious voices like Mom and Dad did when they had something important to discuss and didn't want me to hear.

After the adults had chatted for a little while, they announced that we would be leaving the campsite a day early because the weather conditions were not acceptable enough for additional outdoor activities, which was just fine with me. Thanks to Minne-snow-ta, we got to spend a whole day at the Mall of America, the backup plan I had helped choose. Between the shopping, the amusement park, the aquarium, the movie theater, and the food court, there was something fun for everybody.

At the very end of the day, Olivia, Hannah, Hannah,

and I were resting on a bench when I noticed a mega-cute purple sweater hanging on a mannequin in some store's window display.

"Let's go in!" I said, and we did. I grabbed a sweater from the pile next to the mannequin and headed straight for the dressing room. We all went in the one huge room together, and I was so excited to be shopping with my friends, getting ready to try on a super-cute sweater, that I didn't even think about the fact that when I peeled off my pink zip-up hoodie, my arms would be there, exposed, in plain sight under the gross artificial store lights. *Whoops.*

Hannah and Hannah's mouths dropped all the way to the floor. I was having so much fun that I totally forgot to be careful with my arms. Hannah and Hannah hadn't seen them in almost a year.

But Olivia hadn't seen them ever.

For a second, she stared at them like she'd seen an alien or a ghost or a mouse running across the mall. She made one of those faces like she was trying to decide if she should scream or just keep standing there with her mouth hanging open.

I looked at my arms. They really didn't look bad at all. In fact, they looked kind of amazing. I had **OKAY** running down my whole left arm, and **AWESOME** and **COOL** were on my right. Plus, there were all the words from the poster. Not trying to brag or anything, but I thought I actually looked maybe more fantastic than I ever had. Now **FANTASTIC** was there, too. And I felt incredible—no itchiness at all.

Finally, Olivia spoke. "Are those, like, tattoos?" she asked, pointing, in case I had no idea what she was talking about. Yeah, right.

"Sort of," I told her honestly. "It's a condition I've had since I was little. No one told you about it?"

She made a face like she was trying on a sweater that was way too tight. "Well, sorta . . . I dunno. I heard some rumors, but I figured if it was real, you'd tell me about it yourself."

"Oh." Now I felt bad. What had I been so afraid of? Olivia wasn't just any old person who didn't know about CAV. She was my *friend*. My real friend who hadn't ditched me for the Loud Crowd even though she totally could have. "I should have told you," I said. "Basically, whenever someone calls me a name—or even if I call myself one—they show up on my arms and legs. The nice ones are great, but the bad ones are itchy."

"Whoa," she said in a quiet voice. She stared for a really long time.

"Whoa," Hannah and Hannah repeated.

"Elyse," Olivia said slowly. "This is, like, the coolest thing I've ever seen."

"Really?" I leaned back so I could get a good look at Olivia. She looked like she really meant it and not like she was going to shout *Just kidding!* and burst out laughing. So that was a good sign.

"Sometimes they're not nice words like these," I continued. "Sometimes they're really bad."

"I think they're cool no matter what," she said. "I was surprised at first, but I really think they're awesome."

AWESOME and **COOL** were already on me, but they felt extra good as I let out a huge breath I hadn't even noticed I'd been holding. It felt so good to hear her say that. I was **OKAY** with her or without her, but I'd rather be with her.

• • •

On the way back to the bus, Ami was being her usual noisy self.

"I had such a fab time at the mall," she said loud enough so everyone in Minnesota could hear her. "I bought the cutest clothes. And I hung out with the coolest people. Like, no weirdos at all."

She was probably saying that to me, but I barely heard. That's what happens when you're surrounded by your own friends and your own happy thoughts.

Before I could think about what I was doing, I broke

away from Hector, Olivia, Andy, Layla, and JaShawn, walked up to Ami, and tapped her on the shoulder.

"Question," I said.

Her face looked like she smelled something gross, but I ignored it and went on talking.

"Mr. Todd put me in charge of choosing some music to listen to on the way home, but I'm not sure what's most popular. I was thinking maybe you could decide."

She glared at me for a second, but then her face softened. "Well, I am way better than you at knowing what's cool," she said.

"Yeah." I nodded. "Sure. So you'll be in charge of it?"

"I'll be in charge of it," she said.

"Thanks."

I knew she liked getting her compliments—who wouldn't?—but maybe sometimes the words weren't enough. You couldn't just read them; you had to feel them, too. Mysterious notes, a fancy title, and a crazy wilderness adventure had helped me really understand my words. I couldn't give those things to Ami, but I could definitely give her control of the music.

As my friends and I boarded the bus, I glanced her way. She was talking to Mr. Todd and the bus driver, and she was grinning from ear to ear.

It was just music. But maybe, for her, it was a lot more.

31

SILLY

Dear Elyse,

I just got back from the trip, and it was awesome. But let's get down to business. You don't have that much time left in sixth grade, and this is what you need to do:

1. Survive being in Ms. Sigafiss's class.
2. Figure out Liam's deal, once and for all.
3. Come up with more opinions on things like nail polish colors and bras, just in case Jeg invites me somewhere with her friends and I have to answer more difficult questions.
4. Do stuff. And maybe think about stuff, too. Or think about stuff and don't do stuff. It

might be okay to just do whatever feels right. I think.

5. Find out who wrote the rest of those notes!
6. And one more thing. You might need to break up with Nice Andy.

Catch ya later,
March Elyse

• • •

I closed my notebook and started to unpack when Dad called for me from downstairs.

"What's going on?" I asked. Dad was sitting at the big brown dining-room table with his hands folded. He looked like he was trying to sit really still, but a few of his fingers kept popping out and tapping against each other.

"Hey." He looked up. "Sorry to pull you away from your unpacking. I know how much you love putting things away."

We both giggled nervously. Why was this so awkward?

"So . . . what's up?"

"Um . . ." Dad twiddled his thumbs. "Mom thought I should tell you . . . No, I mean, I wanted to tell you . . .

Well, what you did on your trip, rescuing yourself like that, staying calm under scary circumstances . . . was really brave. And I'm very proud of you."

I don't know what it was about what Dad had just said, but my smile stretched all the way across my whole face. Dad hadn't said something this awesome to me, well, *ever*.

"Yeah, I'm a born explorer," I said with a little laugh.

"Ha!" Dad did a real giggle this time, not a nervous one. It was *sooo* cool, laughing with my dad. "You're silly."

Dad's face turned white as he gasped and threw both hands over his mouth like he had said something absolutely terrible. I burst into an enormous fit of giggles as **SILLY** popped up on my elbow. It really, really tickled!

"That didn't bother you?" Dad's eyes got as big as pizzas.

"No." I gave him a funny look. "*Silly* isn't the worst thing I've ever been called, Dad. I'm in sixth grade."

Before I knew what was happening, Dad got up from the table and smushed me into a gigantic hug. The kind of hug where you can't breathe but you don't mind at all.

When the hug ended and we pulled apart, I asked, "Is that why you never talk to me about anything important? You think you'll call me silly and I'll die?"

Dad laughed, but his face was serious. "Elyse, do you remember the very first word that ever made you itch?"

"Of course," I said. "Poopyhead."

He sighed. "No. No, it wasn't. It was when you were two. We were playing together and you accidentally knocked over a vase that was really important to me because it belonged to my mom, your grandma, whom you never got to meet. I knew you didn't do it on purpose, but I was upset, and in the heat of the moment I scolded you, saying you were a bull in a china shop." Dad took a deep breath. "Since the bad name was a phrase instead of a word, it took up almost your whole two-year-old arm. You were miserable. Screaming bloody murder. Throwing yourself on the ground. Kicking. Sobbing. We took you to the emergency room and they had to give you a shot to calm you down. You started seeing Dr. Patel a lot more frequently after that. And I . . . I was scared of accidentally calling you a name that would hurt you or, you know, literally scar you for life, so I decided that I'd avoid talking to you about anything that could get too serious or personal." He chuckled. "Mom's been trying to get me into therapy for years. I don't know. Maybe it's time. I hate being someone you only talk to about traffic and the weather."

I took a breath as all of this sank in.

"You called me a bull in a china shop?" I raised my eyebrows in a joking-mad kind of way.

"Yeah." Dad sighed.

"Dad . . . I *am* a bull in a china shop. I can be super clumsy. Everyone is, sometimes."

Dad looked scared, but I made an extra effort to stay calm. We both watched as **BULL IN A CHINA SHOP** and **CLUMSY** popped up near my shoulder.

"I'm okay, Dad. See?" I smiled. **BULL IN A CHINA SHOP** and **CLUMSY** itched like small mosquito bites did. A little annoying, but not that bad. Nothing I couldn't handle.

Dad got a huge grin on his face and pulled me into another hug.

"I love you," he said. "For who you've been, who you are, and who you'll be. You're wonderful in every way, Elyse."

"Thanks," I said. "You're pretty cool yourself."

As I climbed up the stairs after our hug, I turned back to look at Dad. He had a goofy look on his face, kinda like he had just read a mushy-gushy greeting card and was about to cry in a happy way.

I felt a little like happy-crying, too.

When I got upstairs, I had a text from Nice Andy.

How R U 2nite! U looked so lovely at school 2day! ☺ ☺ ☺

Yikes. Lovely? He was running out of compliments if he had to go to lovely. It sprang up on my wrist right in between **AWESOME** and **COOL**. It was nice, but I didn't really need it. Like, I was totally good with **AWESOME** and **COOL** and **OKAY** and all the others.

And I didn't even need Nice Andy to get those, because I felt that way about myself.

32

OPERATION DUMP NICE ANDY

THE NEXT DAY AT SCHOOL, I TOLD OLIVIA THAT I WAS going to break up with Nice Andy.

"But he's so nice!" she argued.

"But lots of things are nice," I said, and showed her the list I had made to prove it.

Things That Are Nice Besides Nice Andy

1. Candy.
2. Books.
3. Chapstick that sort of looks like lipstick if you use your imagination.
4. Fuzzy green socks (and all socks, for that matter).
5. Cupcakes.
6. Laughing with your mom and dad.

7. Rescuing yourself from the Minnesota wilderness.
8. Grilled cheese.
9. Making Ms. Sigafiss make grilled cheese after she thought she was done making grilled cheese. Also, soup! Mmm, soup.
10. Lists.

"Wow, there are a lot!" she said. "Can I make one, too?"

I gave her a piece of paper from my notebook. A few minutes later, we taped Olivia's to mine and made a giant list. Hers said:

1. Puppies.
2. Kittens.
3. Rainy days.
4. Sunny days.
5. Things that turn your mouth blue (Popsicles, Ring Pops, etc.).
6. Ice cream.
7. Friends.
8. Brothers and sisters.
9. Dancing awkwardly.
10. The Mall of America.

“What are you guys doing?” Jeg’s head poked out from behind a wall. I hadn’t even noticed her watching us. Her face was covered in slimy-looking clear stuff, like she had gone to get a drink and missed her mouth. Or maybe it was just a weird new colorless lipstick. Maybe it was a fashion statement. I wasn’t sure, so I kept my mouth shut.

“Making a list of nice things,” I said. “Want to do one?”

“Totes,” Jeg answered, and I gave her a piece of paper. Soon, our list grew even longer.

1. Parties.
2. Boys.
3. PG-13 movies.
4. Makeup.
5. Sleepovers.
6. Sharing secrets.
7. Playing truth or dare.
8. Hanging out with friends.
9. Clothes.
10. Kissing.

“Kissing?” Olivia and I squealed at the same time. Jeg went red instantly.

“Just this one guy in France earlier this year,” she said. “And Kevin. And . . . um . . . Liam.”

"Liam?" We squealed again.

After my squeal I started to feel a little sad. I had wanted Liam to be my first kiss, but he didn't even want to be my first hand-hold. But when I thought about it, I realized it was probably good that I didn't waste my first kiss on someone who would ditch me in a blizzard. My first kiss was going to be romantic, with someone I liked and who liked me, too.

"Well, he kissed me," she admitted. "Just now, actually. I broke up with him and he seemed upset, so I let him give me a little teeny one to be nice." She laughed. "Guys, I haven't told anyone else yet. It was really disgusting. He, like, slobbered all over my face. He didn't even use my mouth. I've only kissed two other boys, but I'm pretty sure when you kiss someone, you're supposed to kiss their lips, not lick their face."

She looked at me, waiting for a reaction, and—I couldn't help it—I started to giggle.

Soon Olivia started giggling, too, and then Jeg started, and then the giggles turned into real laughs and the real laughs turned into the kind of laughs where we were holding our stomachs and crying and gasping for air and trying not to pee in our pants. I wanted it to last forever.

"He slobbered all over you!" Olivia gasped through her laughter. Tears were streaming down her face.

"He's a slimeball!" I screeched with delight. "Literally!"

"It isn't funny!" Jeg whined, but she was laughing so hard she almost fell off the bench. "I've been slimed!" she cried, and we all laughed even harder.

A second later, Jeg stopped laughing all of a sudden, like she had just realized her face really was covered in slime and we weren't kidding around.

But it wasn't that. Ami stood in front of us, hands poised on her hips, looking the three of us up and down.

"What's so funny?" she asked.

"Oh, we were just making these lists of nice things," I said. "And then Jeg told us a hilarious story. Do you want to make a list?"

She made a face like she was thinking about it, but she shook her head and linked her arm through Jeg's. "Not now. But I do want to hear the story."

"You're gonna freak," Jeg told her.

As the two of them walked off together, Ami looked back at me and smiled a teeny tiny bit. Then Jeg looked back and mouthed "Slime," and that sent Olivia and me into another round of hysterics.

When we finally got it together, I remembered I had a job to do: Operation Dump Nice Andy, or ODNA for short. All I had to do was march right up to his nice face and be all *I cannot. Read. One. More. Text. That. Ends. In. A. Smiley. Face. Or. Exclamation. Point. Good. Bye.*

No problem.

Only, the second I saw him, I knew I was never going to be able to do that. He really was the nicest guy ever. How could I hurt the kind of dude who opened doors for people he didn't even know and picked up garbage that wasn't even his? Nobody did that. I bet that if he had seen my blue note, he would have picked it up just like Mr. Todd did.

Maybe Nice Andy would be a principal someday. Maybe my kids would go to his school. I couldn't break up with my future children's future principal! But Nice Andy was so nice that he probably wouldn't even be mean to my future kids because of what I was doing to him. Ughhh. Maybe I wouldn't break up with Nice Andy out loud. Maybe I would do it with a note.

Andy,

You are so nice but we can't go out anymore. I am moving to Antarctica.

No. I crossed it out. I couldn't give him that.

Andy,

You are so nice but we can't go out anymore. My parents won't let me.

No, that was a total lie. Mom had practically thrown a party in his honor when I told her we were going out. Dad said, "No dating until you're forty," but I bet he secretly liked how often Nice Andy gave me compliments. Finally, I wrote:

Andy,

I don't want to go out anymore, but I want to be friends.

There. Perfect. Done. I ripped it out, stuffed it in my jeans pocket, and made my way down the hall. The hallway was quiet, but noisy thoughts were zipping through my mind.

Don't do it! You will never have a boyfriend again. You can't go to the mall and get a new one. A boyfriend is not a purple sweater you grab off a mannequin!

You're going to hurt his feelings. He's going to spend the rest of his life crying and then he's going to become a murderer instead of a principal and it will all be your fault.

Elyse, you know you need to do this.

But with a note? That's kind of wimpy.

So without thinking anymore, I snatched the note from my pocket and tossed it in the trash, just as Nice Andy noticed me coming.

"Elyse!" he exclaimed, sticking up his hand for a high five. "What is up!"

"Hey," I said. "Listen, Andy . . ." *Do it. Do it. Do it. You can. You're okay. DO. IT!!!!!!* "I don't want to go out anymore. I just want to be friends, okay?" I took a humongous deep breath.

There. It was done.

"Oh!" He raised his nice eyebrows. "Okay!"

"Okay?" I questioned, raising my eyebrows right back. "That's it?"

"Yeah!" he said. "What'd you expect?"

Uh, tears? Murder? A beautiful future as a middle-school principal ruined forever?

Instead of saying that, I mumbled, "I don't know . . ."

"Okay!" He smiled. "Don't worry about it!"

"Okay," I said, but it all seemed way too easy. "You're really not upset? I mean, you only liked me because you're so nice and you felt bad for me about CAV. So this really doesn't hurt your feelings or anything."

Nice Andy stopped walking and looked at me with a very serious, non-smiling face. If I hadn't been so worried about what he was going to say, I would have wanted to take a picture.

"What? I like you because you're awesome and cool."

"You mean my CAV is."

"No," he said slowly. "I mean, when we first started

being friends in kindergarten, my parents told me to be extra nice to you! Maybe I took it a little too far! What can I say, I'm a nice, happy dude!" He shrugged. "But I wanted to get to know you better; that's why I asked you out! I really think *you* are awesome and cool, y'know!"

I looked at his serious face and his big, wide eyes. He was saying what I always kinda suspected but couldn't believe. But I believed it now. And I was pretty sure I always would.

33

MS. SIGAFISS

THE NEXT DAY, ALL OF US BEAT MS. SIGAFISS TO CLASS. It wasn't like her to be late. While everyone else talked and ran around the room, I took out my notebook. It almost wasn't surprising to see the blue paper sitting there in between the pages like it was waiting for me. I was kinda getting used to the notes. Maybe I'd never know who wrote them and they'd just go on forever. It'd be annoying, never knowing, but maybe there are some things you just don't get to know.

Elyse,

This is going to be my last note to you. It's time for me to move on. I've had a tough time this year, too, but writing to you has helped make me feel a little better, so thank you very much for reading.

What? Of course, now that I had accepted that the notes would go on forever, they were ending. My eyes fell to the floor. This was weirdly kind of sad. After everything, that was it? They were just over? And I'd really never get to know who they were from?

I couldn't pay attention to anything going on in the room, even when Frank the Maintenance Guy came in to watch us and started teaching a lesson on how to make a paper airplane that can fly across a whole room without falling.

Ten minutes later, Mr. Todd came into the room. We heard his giant footsteps from a mile away, so everyone quickly ran back to their seats from all over the room. Frank grabbed all the planes and shoved them into his big back pockets. When they didn't all fit, he stuffed some down his shirt, which made all of us explode in laughs. He looked pointy in some seriously funny places.

"Frank has boobs!" Kevin shouted as Mr. Todd opened the door.

"I'm afraid I have bad news," Mr. Todd said, ignoring the boob comment. "Ms. Sigafiss is unable to be your teacher for the remainder of the year."

"YES!" The entire class erupted in loud cheers and screams. He could have told us that *we* didn't have to go to school for the rest of the year and the reaction would've been the exact same.

Mr. Todd cleared his throat.

"So, like, she got fired?" Ami asked as the noise died down.

"No, not at all. She's pursuing a different path, and I for one am thrilled for her. And, in other exciting news, for the rest of the week, you'll have a wonderful substitute teacher extraordinaire who was available on extremely short notice. Please welcome . . ." He looked at the door dramatically, then sprinted outside of it and walked casually back in. "Me. Mr. Todd. At your service."

We all eyed him suspiciously. Sure, he was probably a better teacher than Ms. Sigafiss, but how well did we really know this guy? What did we really know about him other than how he looked like a grizzly bear and loved all things blue?

Although, I thought, *that grizzly bear hair of his sorta helped me out in the snowstorm.*

Maybe Ms. Sigafiss had taught me something, too, I realized. She had taught me to wonder who people really are, because sometimes the person someone shows your parents isn't the same person they show you. And sometimes even the person they show you isn't the person they are.

And with that very thought, it occurred to me that there might be one new note-writing suspect.

34
THE TRUTH

AT THE END OF CLASS, I TOOK MY TIME GETTING MY stuff together while everyone else left the room. When the door opened, I figured it was someone from the next class coming in. But it wasn't.

"I just wanted to pick up a few things I forgot," Ms. Sigafiss said.

"Oh," I said.

I noticed one of her long scarves hanging over a chair, so I wandered over to it, picked it up, and handed it to her. I had never stood so close to Ms. Sigafiss before. On the one hand, it was totally terrifying; on the other hand, I saw something in her eyes I had never noticed before: sadness. And a whole lot of it.

"Thank you," she said. As she reached for it, the bag she was holding slipped from her hand and fell to the floor. Out tumbled a pack of gum, some keys, a wallet, and a red folder stuffed with blue paper sticking out every which way.

Our eyes met quickly, and in that second I had all I needed to confirm my suspicion. It was her. No way. No. Way! It was *her*!

"You?"

"Elyse, I'd like to show you something." Ms. Sigafiss rolled up her sleeve, revealing a small area of skin on her wrist and a thick black smudge. I craned my neck a little bit to see it more clearly.

I gasped.

Holy. High. Heels.

This was no ordinary black smudge.

It was a word.

FAILURE.

Ms. Sigafiss had CAV. And wrote the notes. *Holy high heels.*

I couldn't decide what to say, so I just looked at her, hoping she'd tell me everything I needed to know. But she stayed silent.

"So . . . why?" I finally asked.

"Well, when I was growing up, no one knew what CAV was. I was treated like some kind of freak by everyone I knew—strangers, my so-called friends, even my own family." She paused and pursed her lips like she was trying to decide whether to go on. "When I was eighteen," she said slowly, "I read about a man named Dr. Patel who was doing research at the University of Chicago, and I decided to pick up and move all by myself. It was my only hope."

My family had moved here for Dr. Patel, too, but it's probably a lot different moving somewhere as a baby, when you don't even know where your toes are, than as an adult, when you've got a whole life in a different place.

"Scary," I said. She didn't reply. Getting information out of her was almost impossible, but I tried again. "Was that scary?" I asked.

"It was. He helped me a little, but it's harder when you're older. You get used to being treated a certain way, and you believe that's how you deserve to be treated. So I was a very sad person, despite how I had started using the prescription creams and whatnot." She finally continued without me pressing her, "I started teaching, but that first day, I saw these young faces in front of me and all I could see were the faces of the kids who were so horrible to me growing up. Elyse . . . I wasn't the best teacher to you. Or to any of the classes who came before you."

It was hard not to nod.

"I figured maybe if I could make kids scared of me,

even if they thought negative things about me, they wouldn't say so. At least, not to my face." She laughed a little, and I thought about how I had called her an **EVIL GENIUS** at the fund-raising show. If she had heard, it would have itched her like crazy.

"When Mr. Todd gave me my students' files this year and I read about you having CAV, it broke my heart. You've gotten medical attention since you were young, but I can't imagine life has always been easy. I thought if I could help you out, maybe give you some anonymous suggestions, things I wish I'd have done when I was your age . . . I don't know, maybe your year would be a little less . . . itchy." Her voice trailed off.

"But," I said, "if you knew I had CAV, and you have CAV, why didn't you just tell me? You could have given me suggestions without the anonymous part."

She took a long breath. "I should've, but sometimes it's hard to talk about. Mr. Todd figured out what I was doing a while ago, and at first he was concerned, but then he was supportive once I explained how it was helping you."

"Yeah," I agreed. "You were super helpful. You made me Explorer Leader!"

She gave me a long look, and the corners of her mouth turned up into a smile. "No," she said. "You earned it, Elyse. I just gave you some ideas. You're the one who made it happen. And it was always more about feeling better anyway."

Had I made it happen? All this time, it just felt like I was following directions. But maybe she was right—I'd performed in the fund-raising show by myself. I'd led the planning meetings on my own. I'd gotten myself out of the wilderness. She gave me ideas, but *I did it*, and felt way better about myself in the process. Holy. High. Heels. Maybe she *was* a good teacher after all. The best, really.

"I actually want to thank you," she went on.

Now we were both grinning. I thought of my letters to myself. If I had told myself that I'd be alone in a room with Ms. Sigafiss—smiling—I would have never believed it in a million years. But here we were.

"By writing to you and watching you grow, I realized how much I love helping students individually. That's why I told Mr. Todd today that I'm leaving Whitman Middle so I can go to school to learn to be a counselor. I got into a program and was planning to start this summer, but I decided I didn't want to wait a minute more. Life's too short. If I leave now, I can start spring quarter with other new students next week."

"Wow! That's really cool, Ms. S."

There were so many more questions I wanted to ask her. So many things I wanted to say. But I could tell she was getting antsy. While she was talking, she had been picking up all the stuff from her bag and looping her scarf around her neck.

"It's time for me to go," she told me, reaching for the door handle. "I can't wait to feel better about myself, to be okay. Like you are, Elyse. Thank you so much." And with a quick wave, she walked through the door and left me standing there, jaw on the floor. She just left, just like that. And then she was gone, and that was it.

I wandered out of the classroom in a daze. Ms. Sigafiss had CAV and had written the notes. My head was spinning all over the place. But when I saw Liam perched against a locker out in the hall—all by himself—everything about Ms. Sigafiss cleared out for a second to make way for one major thought: *Get him!*

For once, I wasn't afraid of what might happen or what Liam might think of me. I had broken up with Nice Andy with my voice and not with a wimpy note. I had rescued myself from the wilderness. I had figured out who wrote the blue notes. I was **OKAY**, even if Liam didn't like me or what I had to say.

"Liam," I said in a voice so firm that it even surprised *me*. "We need to talk. Why did you ditch me in Minnesota?"

"I dunno." He shrugged. "I felt like it."

He *felt* like it?

Sometimes I felt like painting the walls of my house with hot-pink nail polish. That didn't mean I actually *did it.*

"Really? That's why?"

He looked down at his feet and tugged at his collar like it was choking him. Was that sweat I saw, too? Was Liam *nervous*? Around *me*?

"No, that's not why. I just got scared after I told you the truth, okay? I didn't want you going around blabbing to everybody that I wrote you that note. I thought if I could get back first, I could tell Mr. Todd that you were saying crazy things, that you were sick from the cold or something. I was going to lead him to you, I swear. I would never have left you out there forever." Now Liam's eyes were big and wide, looking right into mine, like he was worried I was going to storm down the hall and go tell Mr. Todd everything.

Well, I wasn't a tattletale. But I also wasn't happy. He still hadn't said the one thing I wanted to hear: *I'm sorry.* But the truth would have to be good enough.

And finally throwing away that stupid gum later wouldn't hurt, either.

35
A SPECIAL ONE

AS SOON AS I GOT HOME FROM SCHOOL, I TOLD MOM WHAT I had learned about Ms. Sigafiss, and we rushed off to Dr. Patel's office.

"Well," he said after I divulged my discovery. "I cannot confirm or deny that, but it is, perhaps, slightly possible that you may or may not be on to something."

It still didn't make sense. "Why wouldn't she just be really nice all the time?" I asked. "People would've called her good names instead of bad ones, and then she could be happy."

"But that's not a guarantee," Dr. Patel said. "Just look at you."

I rolled up my sleeves and pant legs. My limbs were decorated with mostly awesome words, but there were still a few bad ones hanging on. **BULL IN A CHINA SHOP.**

CLUMSY. SLOWPOKE—from yesterday when I wasn't walking fast enough in the hall for some seventh grader's liking.

Maybe there would always be something to itch.

I thought about Dad, and how upset he was over the mistake he made so many years ago. You could probably call Dad a **WORRYWART**. I wondered if he thought of himself that way. Even if the word wasn't on his body, maybe it was written in his mind. Maybe everyone had itchy words in their minds, sometimes. Even Liam and Andy and Jeg and Ami. Just because you couldn't see the words didn't mean they weren't there.

"Acting the way she did may not have inspired compliments, but it may have ensured that no one insulted her to her face, either. If your teacher is the other person, that is," Dr. Patel said.

He was right. We all thought she was weird, but no one would dare say so to her face.

"Being afraid of bad names is no way to live," I said after a minute. "She's so much older than me. How do I know that but she doesn't?"

"People deal with things in their own time," he said. "She may not be ready to face it yet. Does this mean that you're no longer afraid of bad names, Elyse? Sixth grade is only the beginning, you know. I'm afraid you're still in for some obstacles."

"Well," I said, "I think there's always going to be something itchy on me. But it doesn't have to ruin my life every time."

"Hmm." Dr. Patel went over to his computer and typed in a few things. "You're an interesting case, Elyse Everett. And a very special one."

"I hope Ms. Sigafiss figures out someday that she's a special one, too," I said.

"So do I," Dr. Patel replied. "So do I."

36

SHORT SLEEVES

Hey girl,

Ever since Ms. Sigafiss left, I've been thinking a lot about the **me** I really am and the **me** other people see. Ms. Sigafiss helped me understand that both things exist. She would always be nicey-nice to our parents, like she was the best friend and teacher ever in the history of friends and teachers, and then she'd be all mean and scary with us.

But she also had CAV. And acting the way she did was how she chose to deal. She was protecting herself in the only way she knew how.

I think I might be a little like her. I acted like a doing person when I was around other people, but I secretly wanted to be a thinking person (and I kind of was, when I was by myself) because that's the real kind of person that I am, even though that person likes to eat lunch in the bathroom sometimes and do a whole bunch of other things that most people find super weird.

I've been thinking about it, and people can just be one person, too, like Mr. Todd. No matter who he's with, he's always talking about blue stuff and making us laugh without trying to.

I don't know what he's like when he goes home after school, but I bet he goes home to a whole house filled with blue furniture, and he probably makes his mom and dad and friends laugh a lot.

The good news is, I think I can mix being a doing person and being a thinking person and be one super-awesome person who thinks and does. And I can be the kind of person who eats lunch with people sometimes and eats lunch with books and be quiet other times. **And** I can be the person who has AWESOME and COOL and OKAY stamped on her arms no matter what, because I really am all of those things when I let myself just be.

The goal for the rest of the year?

I don't even need to say it, do I?
I know what I need to do.
Go get 'em.

April El

• • •

When I emerged from my room in a light purple short-sleeved T-shirt, cute knee-length dark denim cutoffs, and no socks, Mom almost cried. I stood in front of the full-length mirror in the hall with her right behind me, looking over my shoulder. And I was adorable! For once, my hair was doing exactly what I wanted it to. It was perfectly straight, resting just beneath my shoulders, held back by a sparkly black headband. My eyes had somehow changed from mushy seaweed green into an actual nice green that you'd see on a blossoming tree somewhere in the spring.

Was it possible? I knew I was awesome and cool—but had I also turned, dare I say, pretty?

Mom confirmed it, even though her opinion doesn't really count.

"You look gorgeous!" she said with little tears glimmering in her eyes. "I'm so proud of you, sweetie."

GORGEOUS nestled into a comfy spot on my shoulder. I lifted my head higher and straightened out my back so I was standing up very tall. I felt like I could float all the way to school.

Dad said, "I hope rush-hour traffic isn't too bad this morning." But then he added, "Elyse . . . you really look fantastic. Mature and grown-up and absolutely beautiful."

A huge grin spread across my face as the good new words sprang up all over the place.

"Thanks, Dad."

Mom snuck around us and went upstairs. I thought she was going to come back with a sweater for me in case of an itchy emergency. Dad and I went into the living room and sat down.

But she didn't come back with a sweater. She came back with fifteen zillion tubes of goopy cream in a big basket.

"Mom," I groaned. "I know we should be prepared, just in case, but this seems like a little much."

"I'm giving these to you," she said, placing the basket in my lap. "There's no reason to keep them in my bathroom. You know when you feel like you need it and when you don't, sweetie. Right?"

"Well, yeah," I said, but something was confusing. She was saying one thing, but on the trip she'd acted a lot differently. "Do you really think that? Because you only came on the trip to make sure I put the goop on.

That's why Mr. Todd invited you . . . so someone was there to keep an extra eye on the Explorer Leader. To make sure bad words didn't stop my Explorer Leader-ing and turn the whole trip into a disaster."

"Elyse, no!" Mom's eyes got huge. "Mr. Todd just thought it might be fun for you and me to go together. You know, we're always so stressed, so serious. Always going to doctor appointments. He thought we could use a special getaway."

Looking into her eyes, I realized she was right. We were so serious. If Mom made a this-is-so-fun face, I probably wouldn't even recognize it.

She was right about another thing, too: it had been a *very* special getaway, but not in a way that had much to do with her.

I looked at the basket in front of me. They were all there: the thick kind, the thicker kind, the water-resistant kind, the kind with extra moisture . . .

I felt Mom's gaze, and it occurred to me that maybe I had something to give her, too.

"I'm not mad at you, you know," I said. She raised an eyebrow. "Because of the CAV gene. It's not your fault. And it's fine, having CAV. I'm fine. I really am. And I think we should start having more fun together, too. Maybe we could take a trip sometime, just the two of us."

Mom exhaled loudly and enveloped me in a big bear

hug, scattering the creams all over the place. Now that I was looking at her more closely, I could practically see **GUILTY** on her skin. She didn't have CAV, but she still probably had words in her mind—imaginary itches, just like Dad's—that never really went away.

We picked up the creams, but we didn't hurry.

"I think a trip would be great," she said.

I patted her leg, and then we hugged again.

Before I left for school, there was one more thing I had to do. Grabbing my laptop from the kitchen, I plopped down on the couch, went online, and created a new group: **I Have CAV and It's Okay.**

Maybe I'd be the only member for a while, but I hoped people would join eventually. At least they'd know it was there. That had to help.

When I walked into school a half hour later, arms glistening in the gross artificial school light, I had never felt more ready for anything in my life.

Heads turned and people stopped right where they were—even if they were in the middle of the hallway—to look at me. It was creepily quiet, but there was a lot going on. Fingers pointing. Mouths whispering. Bodies huddled. Everybody staring.

"I remember those words," I heard someone whisper.

"That's what Ami was telling us about," someone else hissed.

"That's the quiet girl from elementary school with that disease! SNAV? FLAV?" another person said.

"CAV," I replied. The girl's face got red, like she didn't realize I had heard her.

Someone came up behind me and poked my arm.

"Ouch!" I yelped. That poke would have hurt anyone, words on arm or not.

"What's up with this creepy person?" the guy asked the crowd.

CREEPY popped up before their eyes. I scratched it once, but then made myself drop my hands at my sides.

"Whoa. Creepy," he said again. **CREEPY** got a little bigger and throbbed a little more.

"WHOA! CREEPY!" he yelled, and a bunch of kids came over and laughed. **CREEPY** got bigger and itched even more. Now it was at the level of itchy that definitely demanded cream. The serious goopy kind of cream that I had left at home.

Take a deep breath, I told myself. You're not creepy. You're okay. It's okay.

"I have to go to class," I said to the group surrounding me. And I pushed my way right through them. And, surprisingly, they didn't follow me.

Those kids were a little like the Minnesota wilderness, I thought. Tough. They were tough. They tried to break me.

I didn't have to let them.

Olivia smiled at me when I took my seat in Mr. Todd's class.

"Look at you!" she said. "You look so awesome."

"Thanks," I said.

"Elyse!" Mr. Todd greeted me. "Wow, look at those. Incredible. Looking sharp. Not blue at all."

A lot of people turned to look at me. Some whispered to each other and some stared, mesmerized. I held my arms out in front of me and kicked out my legs, kind of like I was doing a magic trick and this was the grand ta-da moment. The sunlight shone on them through the window, making them brighter and better.

"Wow, your arms are awesome!" Hannah B. said.

"Looking very cool!" Andy gave me a thumbs-up.

"Nice legs!" said Mike. Kevin punched him in the stomach lightly and they both started laughing.

"Do they hurt?" Paige asked.

"Nope," I told her. "Sometimes they itch, but I'm okay."

Liam walked up to my desk from the back of the room and dropped a blue Post-it on top of my books. I looked at him, then down at the note, then back up at him again.

"Open it," he said.

I did.

Sorry for everything.

I smiled. "It's okay," I told him.

"Hey, guys! I got my ears double-pierced this weekend," Ami announced to the crowd gathering around my seat. She turned her left ear toward us. Sure enough, there was her regular piercing, and now there was another sparkling silver stud on the cartilage part of her ear.

Just like that, all thirty pairs of eyes, even Mr. Todd's, shifted over to her. But that was fine. Maybe she needed the attention more than I did. I just needed to be. And now that I was out in the open, I really, truly could.

I glanced to my right. Jeg was the only one still watching me.

"You really look good," she said in a whisper. "It's cool that you can just, I dunno, show that to everybody. And not have to follow rules about what you look like and what you wear. And not care what everyone else thinks."

She fiddled with something around her neck, then dropped the charm so it was dangling over her shirt, right where I could see it.

It was the peace sign necklace. *Our* peace sign necklace.

But as quickly as it appeared, she tucked it away.

"Jeg . . ." I was whispering, too. Something about the conversation felt like a secret, and something about that made me feel really brave. "It kinda hurt my feelings when you started hanging out with the Loud Crowd instead of me. And then when you told them about me and Liam at the beginning of the year . . ."

"Yeah, I know . . . I'm sorry." She sighed quietly. "I just wanted more people, you know? And they started talking to me all of a sudden and it was exciting. And my parents started traveling more this summer and not taking me with them as much. Only sometimes. I guess I got kinda lonely."

"But you had me!"

"But I wanted more than you."

That one hit me like a soccer ball to the gut.

"I don't mean it in a bad way," she said. "I just mean I wanted more than one really good friend, that's all."

"But . . ." I paused. "I mean, don't you think it's sorta weird that they started wanting to hang out with you right around the time your parents got even more rich and famous?"

"That was just a coincidence. They like me. And they're really not that bad when you get to know them."

"Oh . . . okay. Well, if you ever wanna hang out again, we can."

Jeg smiled at me, then took out a little mirror from

her purse and did something to her face. When she looked back at me, her expression was totally different. It was like she had been hypnotized into being honest for a second and looking in the mirror had broken the spell. She shrugged and said, "Yeah, maybe. I'll text you sometime. Totes miss you." Then she got up to join the crowd over by Ami's desk.

I hoped that that wouldn't be another text I'd be waiting forever for, like the one Liam promised that never came.

But it might be. And weirdly, that was good enough for now.

"Totes miss you more," I whispered to myself.

37

THE GOOD, THE BAD, AND THE ITCHY

Dear Elyse,

Today I decided to look back at this notebook and read what I'd written. September seems like years and years ago, but it wasn't really. But so much has happened since then.

I wish I could go back and warn myself: Mr. Todd didn't write the notes. Stand up for yourself. Bring an extra flashlight on the Minnesota trip. Don't drink two cups of cocoa before your Saturday-morning walk.

But you know what? I probably wouldn't have listened to my own advice.

Here are the goals you listed in your September letter:

1. **Stop thinking about the folded paper until I can finally open it after class.**
   Fail!

2. **Stop obsessing over Liam, because he is done liking me.**
   Fine, because I am finally over that darn guy. On to the next relationship.

3. **Instead, obsess over boys like Nice Andy who do seem to like me.**
   Or obsess over no boys. It was super fun being liked, but just because Nice Andy liked me didn't mean I needed to like him back. But it's fun having Andy as a really good friend, too. It's so weird how someone's annoying things can turn into funny, cool things if you change how you look at the person. Now I don't mind going to Soup Palace with him, if he asks. And it's pretty fun, in addition to being delicious. Seriously, how do people make beef stew that amazing?

4. **Stop thinking about the folded blue paper until it's time to open it. (But for real this time, because I totally didn't stop the first time I told myself to stop. Have you stopped by now?)**

Nope. Never stopped. I thought about those notes all the time, and the things they wanted me to do—and I was so glad I did.

Also, Future Me, I'm dying to know—is Jeg still your best friend? (Not exactly. But she's not my enemy, either.) **Has Dad spoken to you recently about anything that actually matters?** (Big-time. Now that he's gotten started, he never shuts up. I love it.) **Did Dr. Patel ever find a cure?** (Not yet, but he's working on it. I'm not really in a hurry.) **Did you pass sixth grade?** (Heck yes I did! Well, I will unless I mess something up really bad before the end of the year. But I won't.) **You better have.** (I will!) **We are not going to be here two years in a row. We're just not. No pressure.**

From,
September Self

P.S.: Sooo, what was that little blue paper all about?? (You wouldn't believe it if I told you.)

I know Dr. Patel is right, as annoying as it is to admit. Every movie I have ever seen and book I have ever read has told me that sixth grade is only the beginning, so it isn't just coming from him. By next fall, the confusing boys will probably get more confusing. The snotty girls will probably get snottier. But I'll have to find a way to deal with it, to stay okay through it all no matter what, to take the good, the bad, and the itchy.

I have **no** idea how I'm going to do that.

I guess I'll have to think about it.

Love,

You

ACKNOWLEDGMENTS

IF I HAD A WORD ON MY BODY, IT WOULD BE LUCKY. This book would not have been possible without the support of so many people, and I am incredibly grateful for each and every one of them.

My editor, Susan Dobinick, should be covered from head to toe in **AMAZING** because she truly is, and that doesn't even begin to describe how much I value her insight and enjoy working with her. Thank you to every **INCREDIBLE** person at FSG/Macmillan, in particular, Joy Peskin, Simon Boughton, Morgan Dubin, Beth Clark, Karla Reganold, and Janet Renard. From day one, this team made Elyse and me feel right at home.

Rebecca Sherman, my agent, is **OUTSTANDING**. Her enthusiasm for this book is incomparable, just like her brilliant editorial eye. Thank you also to the **WONDERFUL** Andrea Morrison.

Gail Nall is **SUPER-DUPER** and should probably have a cape because she's basically my hero. I don't know where I'd be now if she hadn't chosen me to mentor for #PitchWars 2013—I probably wouldn't be a published author. In only a month, Gail took me from a girl with a manuscript and transformed me into a real writer who knew how to revise, handle rejection, and eat chocolate like a champ. She continues to be an absolutely amazing role model and friend, and I am so happy to have her in my life.

Kalvin Nguyen, the one and only person to respond to my "Hey, what if there was a girl who had words on her body?" post on the NaNoWriMo message boards back in 2013, is truly **UNBELIEVABLE**. He read this book approximately a gazillion times and consistently gave excellent feedback. Gail helped me a ton during Pitch Wars, but my book never would have been selected in the first place if it weren't for Kalvin's patience, guidance, and overwhelming awesomeness.

My **SPECTACULAR** early readers: Lori Goldstein, Jen Malone, Erika David, and Jeff Chen. Thank you for loving Elyse's story and helping me make it better. You all made a huge difference!

I've had so many **FANTASTIC** teachers and mentors throughout my life—gigantic thanks to Beth Huntley, Kris Lindborg, Tim Moreau, and Rena Citrin for your support and encouragement with my writing and everything else.

WISE Francis Keating, thanks for letting me borrow "The only certain thing in life is doubt." Thanks for all the other wisdom, too.

My **FUN** writing group back in Chicago: Kate, Kasey, Meg, and Christine. I have never had more productive writerly meetings than the ones with you.

The **SUPPORTIVE** Sweet Sixteeners and MG Beta Readers—you guys rock.

CARING Edith Cohn, thanks for your advice on everything from book stuff to dog-training techniques. You're the best!

All the **EXTRAORDINARY** teachers and librarians out there who work so hard to encourage kids to love books, learning, and themselves. Thank you for all you do.

My **FABULOUS** family and friends: AJ, Davi, Rachel, Francheska, Evan, Jess, Keri, and Natalie. Thanks for always being there no matter what.

The **MAGNIFICENT** Gail Rosenbaum, Andrea Wilensky, and Devorah Schlein. Gail, thanks for using your neuroscience-y smarts to help me name CAV; Andie, thanks for making me take egg roll/dog-walking breaks when things got stressful; Devorah, thanks for not playing any pranks on me (yet) related to my writing or this book. All three of you, thanks for being my people.

Finally, my parents, Kathy and David Cooper. There aren't enough good words in the world to describe your support and what it means to me. I love you.

GOFISH

QUESTIONS FOR THE AUTHOR

ABBY COOPER

What did you want to be when you grew up?
An author! Seriously. Ask my old diaries if you don't believe me. I wish I could talk to Younger Me—she would be SO excited that our dream came true!

When did you realize you wanted to be a writer?
Probably by second or third grade. I was always writing.

What's your most embarrassing childhood memory?
I was front and center during a dance recital, and somehow one of my tap shoes fell off my foot and went flying right into the audience! Luckily nobody got hurt or anything, so that was good. Since then, I've always made extra sure to check that my shoes are on tight.

What's your favorite childhood memory?
Getting my dog, Bailey, in second grade. She peed all over my shirt during the car ride home, but I didn't even care. It was true love.

As a young person, who did you look up to most?
My parents, my Auntie Janie, and my Grandma Mimi. I also had some incredible teachers who were amazing role models.

What was your favorite thing about school?
Anytime we got to read, write, or do something creative. I also loved visiting the school library.

What were your hobbies as a kid? What are your hobbies now?
I loved to collect things as a kid—Beanie Babies, Lip Smackers, candles, seashells, you name it. Now I mostly just collect books, although I do still have most of my Beanie Babies! I also like to go for long walks with my dog, do puzzles, play board games, and try to cook without setting anything on fire.

Did you play sports as a kid?
I was on a soccer team for a few years, but I was that kid who would run away from the ball instead of toward it. Not much has changed since then—I was on an Ultimate Frisbee team a couple years ago and I ran away from the Frisbee, too. I think I just like to run around and not get hit by balls/ Frisbees/other people.

What was your first job, and what was your "worst" job?
My first job was running my own summer camp for kids in my neighborhood. I started Camp Cooper the summer after fifth grade, and I did it every summer until I graduated high school. We did art projects, played outdoor games, had story time, and made snacks. It was so much fun! My worst job was working at a different summer camp. This one had a rock-climbing wall, and part of the job was holding the rope at the bottom while kids climbed. I got certified to do it and everything, but I was still constantly terrified that something horrible was going to happen. (It didn't. Whew. But yikes. Never did that again!)

What book is on your nightstand now?
As I write this, there are seventeen books on my nightstand. Yeah, seventeen. I like to have a backup ready if I finish what I'm reading. Or, you know, sixteen backups.

How did you celebrate publishing your first book?
When I first got the news that *Sticks & Stones* would be published, I squealed so loudly that several people came rushing to see if I was okay. (I was a school librarian at the time, and I was *so* not using my indoor voice.) When the book came out, I had a special dinner with family and friends. Then I went on a road trip to see it on the shelves at every bookstore I could. It was a ton of fun (and yes, there was a *lot* more squealing).

Where do you write your books?
In my bed, mostly. My favorite thing is snuggling up in the morning with my dog, my coffee, and my computer. I get a lot done—and I do it all in my pajamas!

What is your favorite word?
Sesquipedalian. It's a big word that means *a big word*. How cool is that?! Also, it's really fun to say.

What was your favorite book when you were a kid? Do you have a favorite book now?
My favorite book was *Frindle* by Andrew Clements. I thought it was really cool how one kid made such a huge difference. It made me believe that I could make a difference, too. It's hard to pick a favorite now—there are so many books that I love! *The Westing Game* by Ellen Raskin is one that I've read a million times without ever getting sick of it. I love all the unique characters and how the author keeps you guessing. I

feel like every time I read it, I catch something that I hadn't noticed the time before.

What's the best advice you have ever received about writing?

I love the advice that all a first draft needs to do is exist. That's it! It doesn't have to be amazing or even a little bit good. Sometimes I get caught up in wanting things to be perfect immediately, but that's not how writing (or life) works. It takes time to figure out your story, develop your characters, and make every element the best that it can be. It's important to accept and enjoy that process. A first draft is a great way to get all your thoughts and ideas out of your brain and onto the paper. Once you have that very basic foundation, you can revise until it shines. But you can't revise a blank page.

Do you ever get writer's block? What do you do to get back on track?

Of course! I think writer's block is natural and happens to everybody from time to time. For me, it works best to step away from my story and do other things—walk the dog, eat a cupcake, have some adventures—and clear my mind a little. If I'm struggling with something in a story, the answer usually comes to me when I'm not thinking about it at all.

What would you do if you ever stopped writing?

I don't think I could ever stop writing! Even if no one wanted to publish another book I wrote ever again, I would still write because it's something I love to do.

Do you have any strange or funny habits?

I can make this weird humming noise out of my nose (it sort of sounds like a combination of a mosquito and a siren), and

I tend to do it a lot. I like to do different songs. I can even "nose rap," as I call it. Sometimes I don't even realize I'm doing it! I'm pretty proud of it. Once I even won a contest for people with strange talents.

What would your readers be most surprised to learn about you?

A lot of people are surprised to learn that I'm a huge introvert. When you meet me in person, I'm pretty bubbly and outgoing. And while I have a lot of fun being around people, I need lots of quiet time by myself.

She can see people's thoughts in bubbles above their heads.
But is the ability to read thoughts a gift or a curse?

Keep reading for an excerpt.

1
IMAGINARY LOCKS

THE LOCKS WE USE TODAY WERE INVENTED BY A GUY named Linus Yale in 1848, but his son, Linus Yale Jr., made a way improved version in 1861. He was like, *Great invention, Dad, but I know how to make it better,* and that's exactly what he did, and then his dad was like, *Awesome, thanks.*

History is full of cool facts like that. Real life, not so much.

The awesome thing about historical facts is that they're really easy to learn. You can get them from school, obviously, but also from books or the Internet or TV, and there's no end. You can learn as many facts as you can cram into your brain. Then, when your mom says things to you at night like "stay in bed" even though you're twelve and it's a weird thing to say, in your head, you can be like, *Alaska was purchased from Russia in 1867,* and it almost drowns her voice right out. And when she pulls your tie-dye covers all the way up to your neck, and you look really close at her eyes and realize there are tears in them, you can roll away from her and think, *Iceland has the world's oldest democracy.*

And when she says, "I love you, Sophie"—well, that part is okay to listen to, because that's a fact, even if she has a funny way of showing it.

I rolled back around so I was facing her. "Love you, too," I said.

Another fact. I really did love her, but after almost four months, this bedtime routine was getting a little old. And depressing. Definitely depressing. Like the kind of depressing where the teachers who promise never to give homework on the weekends give homework on the weekends. But since it was mostly my fault she was like this in the first place, I just had to deal with it for as long as it went on.

She closed my door and made a clicking sound with her throat, which was supposed to be the imaginary lock she put on it so I couldn't get out.

Imaginary locks were invented in 2017 by Molly Mulvaney, aka Mom.

She put the same kind of lock on the front door to our condo, not when we went *out out*, like to school or grocery shopping or any of the other regular life things we still did, but usually just at night, and usually just for her. Nights were when she got the saddest, when she wanted to go downstairs to the second floor the most and knock on Pratik's apartment door, even though she knew that would be a super awkward, bad thing to do, probably even worse than the time I called Demarius Gilbert last year in fifth grade on New Year's Eve and told him I liked him.

So she pretended she was locked in, and I was locked in with her.

And that was fine with me, mostly. I didn't have anywhere to go. It was late enough that my best friends, Kaya and Rafael, were probably in bed, too, and it wasn't like we could go out for pancakes or anything. So when Mom put the imaginary lock on my door, I left it there, and I didn't go downstairs to Pratik's apartment (because we both knew that's what she *really* meant by "stay in bed"), and she didn't, either, and maybe my not going downstairs somehow helped *her* not go downstairs, and maybe that was a good thing. I definitely owed her a good thing or two.

But maybe, I was starting to think, it wasn't so good after all.

What was so wrong about seeing Pratik? He and Mom had gone out for almost two years, so he was practically family and we missed him a lot, even though they broke up four months ago, not long after school started. Just because he and Mom weren't together anymore didn't mean we had to be "stay in bed" about it.

Maybe if I could figure out how to help her, this weird bedtime ritual could end. I pulled back the covers and sat up straight. The problem was, there was only one person I knew who could help me figure Mom out, and that person was Pratik.

I got out of bed.

Maybe Mom's imaginary lock invention wasn't perfect. Maybe, like Linus Yale Sr., she needed her kid to make a few improvements.

Maybe imaginary locks were meant to hold firm only sometimes.

Other times, maybe they were better off broken.

2

DOWNSTAIRS

I THREW ON MY BATHROBE AND CAREFULLY TURNED MY doorknob. If my imaginary lock had been a real lock, it would have probably made some weird clicky noise, totally waking up Mom and getting me in a ton of trouble.

I peeked around the corner to make sure Mom's door was closed, tiptoed out of my room, and inched toward the front door.

Part of me expected some scary loud alarm to go off as I grabbed my key and opened the door. But I went out into the hall and nothing happened except for my stomach feeling as twisty as the garlic knots Mom and I had eaten with our pizza for dinner.

Mom used to call us the Adventurous Girls. We used to *be* the Adventurous Girls before and during the time she dated Pratik. It used to be a no-brainer to order the hottest, spiciest garlic knots on the menu. It used to be a no-brainer to do any of the fun, adventurous things we did: getting off the bus at random stops and exploring new neighborhoods, taking flying trapeze lessons by the lake, trying every different ride at the state fair, even the really fast ones and the upside-down ones and the ones that flung you into freezing cold water . . . but all of that was before. Now we had to try to talk ourselves into doing stuff like that, but we didn't try that hard. Mom would be like, "You want to?" and I'd shrug and be like, "Do you?" and she'd shake her head and we'd go back to watching our movie on TV or whatever and that would be it.

The truth was, we only had garlic knots tonight because there was some deal where they came with the pizza for free. I only ate one. Mom only had a bite. We threw the rest away.

I paused before I took the final two steps to get to the second floor. This was where Mom and I used to stop for our typical Stairway Selfie. We'd smile and snap a shot or two or ten with one of our phones, just to make sure our hair was good, nothing weird was hanging from either of our noses, and we were both still looking as cute as we had when we'd left our place.

After all, it was at least a twenty-second walk from our condo to his. A lot could change in twenty seconds. I knew that better than anybody.

Twenty seconds was all it took for me to ruin Mom's life the first time.

And another twenty seconds to ruin it a second time with Pratik.

But maybe a third twenty seconds could fix it.

The garlic knot in my stomach felt bigger and knottier as I reached Pratik's door. I needed to be brave for Mom. This was not even a scary thing I was facing. This was a door.

I brought my knuckles to the wood, tapping twice, softly, and then stood back and waited, but no one answered. I glanced down at my Minnie Mouse slippers. What was I expecting, anyway? That Pratik would open the door, see me, and magically remember how much he cared about us and how much fun we had together? That he would come upstairs so Mom could be happy again?

When the Revolutionary War was going on and the colonists lost their first few battles to the British, they were pretty bummed out. They started thinking maybe all those rules and taxes and stuff wouldn't have been so bad after all. They felt totally silly. And standing in the hallway with no one but Minnie Mouse to keep me company, that's how I felt, too—maybe Mom invented the lock rule for a reason.

After waiting for what seemed like a thousand years (or at least until ten-thirtyish, which I knew it was because if I'm still awake at ten-thirtyish at night, my eyelids get droopy and my cheeks feel weirdly sore), I decided to do the only other thing I could think of: go outside. Pratik didn't always answer his door, but he usually left his shades wide open.

I crept down the stairs to the first floor (Ms. Wolfson's floor), and then opened the door that led outside. I pulled my fuzzy blue bathrobe closer to my skin. Chicago winters seriously don't mess around. Maybe a coat would have been a good idea. But I wouldn't be out for long. Just long enough to see if he was home and maybe figure out a way to get him to answer his door.

I hurried to the giant tree in front of our building and hid behind it. Then I slowly peered out, my droopy eyelids in full swing, and forced those droopers up. Pratik's light was on. He was totally home. I knew it.

He was sitting at his table, holding a fork and eating something that looked pretty fantastic. That was one of the awful things about Pratik—he was an incredible cook. Well, now it was awful, since we didn't get any of the food anymore. Even now, in the middle of the night, just thinking about his amazing spicy curry and naan and tandoori chicken made my mouth water up a storm. Oooh, and his spaghetti with the fancy turkey meatballs. And his chicken enchiladas. And his—

Okay, I had to focus.

The rest of the neighborhood was eerily quiet. Even on a Tuesday night in February, there was usually something going on in Wicker Park. Our condo was right off Milwaukee Avenue, where all the restaurants and stores were. But tonight, I could only hear the rustle of the wind. *Go back inside, you weirdo,* it seemed to say. This was a bad idea.

So I took one last look at Pratik and glanced toward the front door, figuring out how I could run back in without him seeing me or tripping and falling on my face. But maybe it would be good if he saw me. I guess I had the same problem Mom did when it came to Pratik—sometimes I wanted to see him and be seen, and other times I would do *anything* to make sure I was hidden away. It was usually one or the other, and whatever the feeling was, it was always really, really strong.

I tugged on the strings of my bathrobe so it wouldn't come loose and fall off during my attempt at a sprint, and then I peeked up one final time. *I'm down here, Pratik. I'm down here, whatever yummy-looking greenish-tannish thing of deliciousness you're eating without Mom and me.*

Poor Mom. She would probably love a greenish-tannish thing of deliciousness right about now. And she couldn't have one.

Pratik didn't look out the window. But wait—what was that? I scrunched up my eyebrows and tried to see closer. There was some sort of whitish bubbly thing hanging over him, like a funny-looking hat that wasn't actually attached to his head.

I tilted my head to the side. It had to be at least ten forty-five by now; I was probably losing my mind a little bit. This was super-duper-droopy-eyelid/weirdly-sore-cheek territory.

But was I really losing it? The thing definitely looked like a bubble, like the kind you see in cartoons with the three little dots coming out of the character's head leading to a big bubble where you can see their most private thought, the thing they're really thinking but can't (or won't) say out loud.

The big bubble, I was 99 percent sure of it now, was hanging over Pratik's head like it was no big deal. And, even freakier, there were words inside it, slowly appearing one by one. Words!

I squinted my eyes to read them.

Man, this food is amazing. I'm such a good cook! I wish Molly and Sophie were here to try this.

Just as soon as I read the words, they disappeared. What. The. Holy. Chocolate. Pancakes.

I froze to the ground, my eyes suddenly wide open and not droopy at all, as I tried to make sense out of what I had seen. The bubble was still there, but the words had disappeared after I read them. Maybe I had actually fallen asleep an hour ago and this was some sort of crazy dream. Maybe that spicy garlic knot had done something besides set my mouth on fire. Maybe . . . I didn't know.

But I knew for sure that this going-outside—going-*downstairs*—business had been a terrible idea. Now, with these freaky bubbles, things were even *more* confusing.

At the same time—he missed us! He really missed us!

I snuck back into the building, took the elevator up, opened the apartment door, slipped into my room, threw my bathrobe on the floor, and dove into bed, pulling the covers all the way up to my neck the way they were before, the way they should have stayed before I got my crazy idea and was rightfully punished for it with more craziness. I shouldn't have done that. I should have stayed right here. Why couldn't I do anything right? I'd messed up so much stuff for Mom. The least I could do was listen to her when she said to stay in bed, and I couldn't even manage that.

After what felt like forever, my heart slowed down, my eyes closed, and I convinced myself that there was no way I could have actually seen what I thought I saw. There was no way. Cartoon people had thought bubbles hanging over their heads. Real people didn't.

Unless . . . unless, somehow, they did.